A KINGDOM

LIBRARY OF WALES

James Hanley was born in Dublin in 1901 and grew up in Liverpool. He saw active service in the navy during First World War and was briefly in the Canadian Army. His literary career began with the publication of *Drift* in 1931, which was also the year he moved to Wales, and was followed by *Boy* in 1932 and later a sequence of five novels set in working-class Liverpool. He lived first in Merionethshire and later at Llanfechain in Montgomeryshire, where he developed a friendship with the poet R.S Thomas who dedicated a book to him. He wrote prolifically throughout a long career and his output includes novels, short stories and plays. He moved to London in 1964 but continued to regard Wales as his home. He died in 1985.

A KINGDOM

JAMES HANLEY

PARTHIAN
LIBRARY OF WALES

Parthian
The Old Surgery
Napier Street
Cardigan
SA43 1ED

www.parthianbooks.com

The Library of Wales is a Welsh Government
initiative which highlights and celebrates Wales' literary
heritage in the English language.

Published with the financial support of
the Welsh Books Council.

www.thelibraryofwales.com

Series Editor: Dai Smith

A Kingdom first published in 1978
© Estate of James Hanley
Library of Wales edition 2013
Introduction © Neil Reeve
All Rights Reserved

ISBN 9781908946539

Cover Image: Haystack, Ty Mawr III by Harry Hughes Williams
Cover design: Marc Jennings

Printed and bound by Gwasg Gomer, Llandysul, Wales
Typeset by Elaine Sharples

British Library Cataloguing in Publication Data

A cataloguing record for this book is available from the British Library.

INTRODUCTION

An elderly farmer has just died, following an accident on a remote mid-Wales smallholding. That night, his daughter Cadi, his helper and carer for many years, numbed close to vacancy by what has happened, staring into the darker vacancy outside, has a momentary vision of her father and his assistant, long ago, answering the call of their work:

The darkness seemed to vanish with a mere closing and opening of the eyes, and there before her lay the green fields, and she saw moving across them two close together men, their heads slightly bent, as they went forward to deal with the last of the first hay. So, rooted at this window, she was looking into another day and another time, and watching men walk on, closest to all they knew, was real, and would never end.

There are so many complex feelings in this elegiac evocation of hill-farm life: feelings about authenticity, and meaning, and moral anchorage, and at the same time an undertow of exhausted resentment at nature for so remorselessly imposing its rhythms, subduing differences, creating almost a tacit battlefield camaraderie in the heart of apparent peace – bent heads, mowing, the unquestioning onward step. From its very first line, *A Kingdom* is preoccupied with the connotations surrounding the word 'rooted' – 'All is root here, even the silence' – preoccupied with what it means, for good and ill, to be tied to such a place, to its unremitting demands, to the dwarfing massiveness of the mountain looming over one's day, to the dreams of other worlds opened up by the least break in the order of life. It's close to R. S. Thomas territory – literally so, since in the 1950s Hanley had lived a few miles from Thomas's Manafon parish, and they were good friends – territory whose rhythms can so enfold the bleak and the consoling that the two are sometimes hard to distinguish. Perhaps, though, Hanley's characters breathe a marginally freer air? The farmhand Twm Pugh, for instance, has something of Thomas's Iago Prytherch about him, but a Iago unconstrained by the author's wish to have him represent or symbolise an idea about Wales and Welsh life. Instead, there is a simple, touching inwardness in Twm's gauche, helpless, resigned love for Cadi; Twm, once 'the bringer of unwanted bouquets', now moving 'like a shadow' as he helps carry her father's coffin downstairs, 'peering down into the kitchen' he may once have dreamed of possessing.

I find it a remarkably haunting novel, full of images and sentences that resonate and expand in the mind long after reading. Almost as remarkable is the fact that James Hanley was 80 when he wrote it, in 1977. By this time he had long since moved away from Wales, where he had lived for thirty years, firstly at Corwen, then at Llanfechain, near the Shropshire border, where he produced a good part of his dauntingly large output – some 20 novels, plays, volumes of stories, and radio dramas. Hanley was born into a Liverpool-Irish family in 1897. He served at sea (and briefly in the Canadian army) during the First World War, worked at various jobs, educated himself, and began publishing fiction in the 1930s – most notoriously *Boy* (1931), an unsparing account of sexual abuse on board merchant ships, which became the subject of an obscenity trial. He was never a popular writer, but was held in the highest regard by other novelists, including E. M. Forster, V. S. Pritchett, and Doris Lessing; his reputation was for uncompromisingly realistic accounts of working-class life (*The Furys*, 1935), of situations of extreme privation (*The Ocean*, 1941), and for compellingly intense, Camus-like portrayals of alienation and disengagement (*Levine*, 1956). His many admirers have regularly tried to revive interest in him, but with limited success; maybe he wrote too much, too variously, and over too long a period to fit comfortably in the literary pigeonholes. But he could certainly be reclaimed as a Welsh writer; he identified with Wales to the extent not only of making his home there, but of successfully encouraging other Welsh-connected writers to join him and live for a while nearby – John Cowper Powys in the 30s, and during the war the novelist Elizabeth Berridge and her husband Reginald Moore. Admittedly, very little of the vast amount of writing Hanley produced in Wales would directly involve Welsh settings (the main exception being his 1954 novel *The Welsh Sonata*). It was only after he moved to London in the mid-1960s that he began a sustained and deeply-felt creative exploration of the adopted home he had left behind, in several unfinished sketches for stories and plays, and eventually two novels, *Another World* (1972), set on the north Wales coast, and *A Kingdom*, which would be his last completed work; he died in London in 1985.

The substance of *A Kingdom* is the difficult relationship between Cadi and her estranged elder sister, Lucy, Cadi's predecessor in the role of father's helpmeet, who one day, secretly and without warning, fled from the farm to England and marriage, never to see the old man again. Cadi promptly gave up her job as a teacher in Manchester to take Lucy's place in her father's lonely, narrow world, and has stayed in that world fifteen years, her mind and skin alike weathered to it. The novel charts the courses whereby each sister came to be what she now is; the conversations between them, as they prepare for the funeral, flash and glitter with the suppressed awareness on both sides that the decision of the one to get away, her hatred of everything their father made her do, effectively determined the fate of the other, created the pattern of guilt, self-submission, self-reliance, and occluded rage that now directs the younger woman's life. Those wonderfully brittle conversations not only give the narrative its momentum, but offer us, suddenly and in passing, sharp glimpses of the small telling details of the life, the feel of the landscape, the creaking stairs, the condensation-cloud on the tiny kitchen window, the close, warm smell of three cows in a shed: details caught between the gaps and spurts of dialogue, and that seem the more real for being so obliquely noticed.

Curiously, the decision to make the sisters the central focus of *A Kingdom* came very late in the compositional process. Reading Hanley's early drafts, one can find at least six false starts at the novel: it began life as a play (as did much of Hanley's later work), and then changed to two separate narratives gradually blending together, until the real heft of the story finally emerged. Lucy was originally Cadi's aunt, her father's sister rather than her own, an aunt moreover whose rare visits brought colour and warmth to the farm, and who vainly urged Cadi to escape from it. All this seems to have been completely transformed almost at the last minute: a striking example of the role of serendipity in the progress of writing which in its final state seems so assured and authoritative. It's something Hanley himself was well aware of, judging from the jottings in his late notebook of a spoof 'interview' about his methods:

How do you begin a novel?
I don't know. I just begin.
But surely you know what you're going to write about?
I think about it, but not too deeply.
But surely you must plan?
Sometimes – and sometimes I daren't.

In this case, trusting to luck – or not probing one's impulses too deeply – certainly paid off, since the revised conception of the women's relationship brings an intensity and immediacy to the story which none of those early drafts looked quite like realising.

Intensity and immediacy are also partly sustained by the way the novel leaves the origins of the situation largely unfathomed. Exactly why did the father, a blacksmith, abandon his forge in north Wales and choose to move here, to take on a way of life entirely strange to him, and never to speak of his reasons? There are hints of adultery, of unrequited desire – even faint suggestions of incest – but nothing is ever made fully clear: above all, perhaps, the peculiar age gap of more than 20 years between the two sisters, who nonetheless shared a bedroom at the old house, and who remember standing at the forge door together, looking up 'to see their father towering, see the sparks fly, and in due time hear the expected explosion, as the huge beast, now shod, bounded forth as from the bars of a cage'. The violent potency of such images gives the figure of the father an almost mythic, archetypal dimension; indeed, distant echoes of *King Lear* can be heard through the novel – the faithful and unfaithful daughters, an old man's power turning to vulnerability, and, in an inversion of Shakespeare's close, the daughter carrying the father's body, struggling back home with him across the fields, across the kingdom he had ruled over so fiercely.

A tensely mysterious atmosphere like this is often enhanced in fiction by the presence and viewpoint of an outsider, who only knows so much, and whose sensibility is not really adequate to the strange embers of family passion he has stumbled across. Lucy's English husband David, puzzled, sympathetic, slightly complacent, has come, as he believes, to help, as he did all those years ago when he offered Lucy her escape-route. But he never seems conscious of the impact his intervention had on the household – nor, for that matter, of the way Lucy's almost abject dependence on him speaks so eloquently of what her previous life must have been like. He respects the place and its people, but he can't help seeing it simply as a hopeless dead end: 'How far away from everything these people seemed, how hard-working, an utter absorption, the sheer grind of it all'. At one point he tries, mildly enough, to encourage Cadi to take *her* chance to put it behind her and move on:

> "There's always tomorrow," said David... "Well isn't there, for everybody?"
> She seemed to make him wait ages for an answer, and he thought how calm, how final it was. "We remember yesterday," she said.

It is as if in the pause she were weighing up a number of possible answers, each of which would have to shut out as much as it included. And knowing the cost of making it, her commitment nonetheless is to that obdurate, intricate, guarded, precariously-surviving rural Wales, which is as alive in these pages as in any I know.

Neil Reeve

vii

A KINGDOM

JAMES HANLEY

1

All is root here, even the silence, and this was broken only by the distant call of a dog fox, and the hoot of an owl that followed after. A mountain, locked in its own power, seems to accentuate itself, even behind the wreaths of mist that sway and hover. A single light splashes down into the darkness, and there was no sound and no movement in the small top room from which it shone. A securely fastened window shut out the wind's sigh, and the woman sat beneath it heard only the steady drip drip of water in the roof. She sat quietly at the foot of a bed, her hands cushioned in her lap, and stared down at the man in it. The eyes opened and the eyes closed, but he spoke no word. Bed close, she sat on, and listened to the heavy, asthmatic breathing. How long? she asked herself.

At that moment there came to her ears the loud, ringing footsteps of one climbing a mountain road, and she knew it was a man. Suddenly they stopped, and she thought of a knock on the door, but he suddenly went on, the pause indicating the caution that serves height and silence.

One other sat in a chair close beside her, and from time to time she looked up and flung him fugitive glances, but spoke no word. The man sat in his overcoat, and his hat lay on the side of the bed. Once or twice his eye took in the woman's hands, anchored in her lap. They were red hands, blotched, and seeming all muscle, and to him they had a worn and tired look, and he told himself that they were a man's hands. And at last she spoke.

'Well, doctor?'

'I couldn't say, Miss Evans, not now; we just wait.'

'Yes, doctor,' she replied, and gravity forward.

'The fall was incidental, but what followed was not,' he said.

'Yes, doctor.'

And now she looks closely at him, who is doctor and friend and father confessor in a small kingdom, and then, suddenly alert in her chair, looks down once more at the man in the bed, waiting for the moment when the eyes would again open, will see her, know she is there, who was there from the beginning. And the doctor sensed the tenseness in her waiting. Again he glances at the hands, and the fingers suddenly restless where they lie. So he got the measure of one who waited, who would always be taller than her father. He looked at the wealth of black hair, and into the eyes, that in this moment seem to redeem the message engraved upon flesh.

Must be around forty now, he was telling himself. The tiny tick of a clock was heavy in the silence. The chair creaked as he moved.

2

'Good of Edwards,' he said, 'at that time of the night.'

'Yes, doctor.'

He leaned forward in his chair. 'I expect you've telegraphed your sister,' he said, and added quickly, 'Cadi,' which for the first time made the room seem warmer by calling her by the name she was best known.

'I have,' the words flat, hollow.

'Good,' he said.

He looked down at the arms, stiff and stretched on the bedcover, then suddenly noted a change in the breathing, and rising, exclaimed, 'There!'

And Cadi, too, rose, and leaned forward as the eyes opened, as the lips parted, moved, the tongue visible, but it was empty of words, and they still waited. Suddenly she felt the doctor's hand on her arm, and words were warm and close to her ear.

'I think he wants to say something, Cadi,' he said.

So she leaned over the bed, was close as ever she would be, saw the arms move, the lips go wild, gibberish come free, and in the same moment the doctor, too, leaned forward to the man who would not rise from a bed.

'Yes, Father... yes...' the woman said, her mouth close to his ear, her eyes fixed steadily upon him. In an instant a hand was raised in air, a finger moving, beckoning, as though there was something closer than close in the moment, and she waiting, hands clasped, noticing the hairs upon the nose, the grey stubble at chin, and higher, and for the thousandth time to the iron-grey hair that had once been bared in all weathers, and always covered by a stout sack when the wind howled and the rain poured.

'Listen,' the doctor said.

3

The man in the bed spoke, and they listened. Eye met eye. Cadi waited. 'Thank you,' the man said, fell back on the bed, who on opening his eyes had imagined this room to be full of women. And that's it, thought the doctor, as the sound came, as the eyes closed.

He was not quite certain, but he thought the woman had wilted, and then her hand was free, and both were now clapped to her face, and she pressed and pressed as though this was total and final action in a quiet room, on a winter afternoon in the longest month of the year. She watched him make a swift, light movement down from the man's forehead, and then he turned and looked at her, still erect, still stiff, and he wondered when the hands would fall from her face.

'I'm sorry, Miss Evans,' he said, and so quietly that she had to strain for the words. And then her hands came down, and she looked at him who, in this professional moment, enquired, almost casually, if she would like him to call and inform Hughes of Y Fraich, as he passed that way. He saw her hesitation, then reached down for his hat.

'Yes?'

'If you like, doctor, thank you; of course I will see him myself.' After which they left the room, paused for a moment on the short landing, and she preceded him down to the kitchen. And the warmest thing in this hour was the fire that shone brightly and sent their shadows toppling.

'How good you've been to him,' he said, held both her hands, and for the first time offered her a fleeting smile. And had she any idea about the time of her sister's arrival?

'The trains are slow, doctor, two changes on the way, and it's nearly always a long wait at Shrewsbury.'

'Perhaps Mr Stevens will come, too,' he added, encouraging, and yet concerned.

'Might,' she said, and then, 'no, I doubt that; he'd have to get leave from the Post Office, but I can't see it at such short notice.'

'I see.'

'Yes.'

She watched him suddenly dive into pocket after pocket, though what he searched for never came to view, and she wondered what it could be. Glancing through the window she caught sight of his tiny Austin, recalling that years previously he had got about on horseback, as had his father.

'Certificate in the morning,' he said, professional again.

'I understand, thank you,' she replied.

For the third time he extended a hand, and then she followed him to the door, and watched his brisk walk down the long, weed-ridden path to the little white gate. Reaching this, he put a hand on the latch, and then exclaimed quietly upon winter air, 'Never even cried.' A last glance back at the house showed him curtains being drawn. 'It's the way it goes.'

And then he got into his car and drove out of the lane.

'Poor woman,' he said, and accelerated, and thought of the eyes that were dry, the cloud of raven black hair, and the hands in a lap. Later that evening he remarked to his wife upon the thing that seemed strange to him, and she, Marged, listened.

'I'd have searched long for a sign of distress,' he said, 'of shock.' Then, more abruptly, 'Odd she never married.'

'Some quite attractive women don't, dear,' she replied, and went off to prepare the dinner.

5

Cadi went slowly upstairs, and sat on the edge of her father's bed. She thought of the years that had passed her by, as she thought, and remembered the hour when her nearest neighbour, Mari Edwards had sat with her, and, like her, just waited and listened. Watching and waiting. She crossed to the window, and stood there for some time, looking out, hard and constant, yet saw nothing outside, and then bed. She thought of the years that had passed her by, as she exclaimed, 'Gone, gone.' And slowly, almost imperceptibly, certain days of a week were already drawing her clear of this room, and she wandered in them. She walked through a Sunday come and gone, and a Monday that had been trodden through, but Tuesday was suddenly there, with the force of a blow.

My God!

Her father up at the self-same hour, having his mug of hot, strong tea, and leaving the house, but not before informing her that he was going to Paradise Corner to continue with the new staking. So the day struck the room, struck her, and she sat up suddenly and half turned towards the door. She looked down at the man, and suddenly heard the bang of the door, and later, the click of a gate. He had gone. But the day grew, and he had not returned until nearly ten o'clock, had his breakfast, after which he again left the house. Not a word had been spoken, and this was normal in a house where the words were few, and messages often reached her on the wings of a quick glance, and she had answered them, wordlessly. And when he had gone off, she did all the things that she had done yesterday, and the days before that, such days having their fixed rhythm, and she was close to them. So morning had grown to noon. She went out and collected

6

the eggs, looked in at a sick cow, returned to the house and lighted the lamp, carefully trimming its wick. This done, she began the preparation of the evening meal. She replenished the fire, and laid the table, then went out to the back and took down the flitch from the hook, and cut two slices of fat bacon, and after this, the bread and butter. A kettle was singing on the hob. And at last she sat down, folded her hands, and waited.

Afternoon reached evening, and she watched the light begin to go. She went out to the back again and examined the milk, and thought of the butter that must be made. So all the usual things had circled her mind. She stood at the table and looked at the waiting meal. Another glance at the clock, and a quick run to the window to find the darkness full, and deep, and home. A day had come to an end, and her father had not returned. And she began to pace a slated floor, listening to the sound of her own steps, then back to the window again, and staring out, and nothing there, still listening, still wondering, hoping for the sound of a gate, the heavy tread down a long path. Twice she had thrown wide the door and received a rising wind in her face. But no other sound, no familiar footsteps. She covered her face with her hands. And then she saw herself lighting a hurricane lamp, and rushing from the house, with a last despairing look at the clock that had no answer. Over the dark fields, and stopping, and going on, and stumbling, a lamp swinging drunkenly in her hand, mumbling to herself, and this becoming louder as she reached the first gate, and on again, and so to another, where suddenly she halted, as though this were a known compass point. And calling, and listening, and waiting. Then on again, and a spurt down a hill, running, and still wondering, still hoping. Giant shadows of trees rising in her path, and these, under the swinging lamp, seemed moving and overwhelming. And calling again through cupped hands. And she couldn't believe it, and wanted to shout at her loudest, and didn't, but ran madly down the slope, the lamp suddenly loose and bounding down the bank. Darkness. And she ran after the lamp, and finally found it. Miracle, she thought. It had not gone out. And suddenly, there he was, flat on his back, and a new stake tight in his knotted fist. She saw, she heard it all, in a silent room.

Words falling as she leant down and stretched out to raise him up. 'Father! Are you all right; what happened? God, I was worried.'

And his mouth wide, and she waiting for the words. She felt his breath in her face. She listened as he gabbled.

'Fell. Hit my head; couldn't get up; tried twice; fell down again; it got cold after that.'

'Yes, yes, *yes,* what time, Father, what *time?*'

Lips moving and nothing coming out, so she reached threshold of her anxiety, and shouted, 'Time, what time was this?'

And he stuttered, 'I don't know.'

She reached for his vest pocket, and took out the watch, and against the light of the lamp, saw the time.

'You've been lying here nearly four *hours,* Father.'

'I couldn't... move.'

She had put down the lamp, then raised him to his feet, put an arm about him, and picked up the lamp, and cried in a shrill voice that it was all right now.

'It's all *right,* Father, I'm *here.'*

He leaned heavily upon her, and she felt this weight, and once stumbled herself and almost fell, came erect again, held him tight, suddenly swung the lamp, cried into his ear. 'You'll soon be home.'

And louder to night air, 'God! Am I relieved?'

Moving through the darkness, holding him tight, hanging on securely to the lamp.

'Easy, Father, *easy –*' and 'Careful, *careful.'*

The weight growing, and again halting, putting down the lamp, thinking, I'll have to *carry* him, and struggling on, and in an instant letting go of the lamp that rolled down a bank, and this time, went out. And she cursed it.

'I'll *carry* you,' she said.

'I... I...' and a bout of coughing.

As she raised him over her shoulder she could barely glimpse his face. And silence. Had he fallen asleep? Was he dead?

'*Father!*' and shaking him, 'Father.'

Halting again. 'Are you all *right?'*

The answer was an incoherent mumbling, so she went on, and only once sat down on a bank. Holding him tight, and always listening, then crying into the air, 'If only there was somebody.'

How far was it. How soon?

Struggling upright again, stumbling on, watching, hoping for the sight of another gate, the familiar lane, a known hedge, and a light streaming down the path, and in that very moment, staggered into it. The path itself seemed peopled by shadows.

'You all right, Father?'

Another halt, and no answer, after which she seemed to hurl herself home.

The light and the door, crashing it in, the chair, falling with him at the foot of the stairs, and then the slow drag upwards, kicking in another door. At last. Undressing and getting him to bed, rushing below for water and towel, bathing his face and hands, whispering in his ear, words spilling out, and now she heard them again, loud and clear in her head.

'There, Father. You're all right now; you're home,' and a sigh of relief.

Looking down at him, flat on his back. The stairs again, fussing in the pantry, and back again, holding him up, pouring the warm milk into his mouth, waiting for a move, a sign, and the thought already winging its way beyond the house.

Must see Mervyn, must, the words as signals, facts.

He *had* fallen, he *was* ill. It was real.

And she sat on in the chair, listening to a known, an old sound, a drip in the roof. How loud it suddenly seemed, and sitting there, listening to it.

I never felt so alone as I do now. Do hope Mari can manage it.

So she was back in the hour when they had both sat by his bed, remembering how a stricken man had tried to sit up, then fallen heavily back, an arm in the air, a finger moving, a violent stuttering. She thought of the mystery and horror of it.

'In the canister downstairs,' her father said.

The canister downstairs, its contents the history of Pen y

Parc days. She glanced up at this, and at the smaller one at the other end of the chimney-piece, and then her eye focussed on a small stone horse that stood between them. It was as though she were looking at this for the first time, and she smiled, remembering an occasion. An unexpected visitor. How long ago was that? And she fretted about not remembering, but the smile stayed, since she had always loved this ornament.

I wish Mari would come.

Yesterday had flown, and tomorrow seemed deserts away. She asked herself why she had been unable to cry.

I couldn't.

She thought of Mari and her husband, Mervyn, her nearest neighbours, remembering her three-mile walk, after that other walk. Hammering on the door, in the night, seeing the window open and Mervyn calling out.

'It's me.'

And the voice recognized, and how quickly he had come down.

How good he was, cycling away at once for the doctor. But they had both been kind, so thinking of them, she felt happy for them. So happy in themselves, and their life together. What on earth would she have done without them? The deep tones of the grandfather clock struck the hour, and she turned to look at what she always thought beautiful, remembering the last time her father had wound it.

Poor Father, and something came to an end.

She jumped when the knock came to the door.

'Why, Mervyn!' she said, and he followed her into the house. 'Do sit down.'

Mervyn, breathless, spoke. He had been in the Post Office,

11

and Mrs Pugh had given him a telegram. She opened and read it.

'It's all right, Mervyn, Lucy's coming. Thank you again.'

'How's Geraint?'

'Welcome,' he said.

'Fine, a letter this morning; yes indeed, he's well.'

'I'm glad.'

As he went out she caught the glance he had so often extended to her, who, like his wife, had often wondered why she had never married. The door closed.

I want to see Lucy, she told herself, and yet somehow, I don't.

In a flash she had forgotten her, thinking only of a man just gone, and of their son doing so well at school.

Strange seeing her again, so long ago, and she supposed her sister was happy. Wonder what he's like? she asked herself, suddenly trying to remember his name, and then it came. David. Of course. Wonder if he'll come, too?

She began pacing the kitchen, crossing to the door, listening, pacing again. Hope she won't be long, never felt so alone before, never. I'm nearly forty now, she thought, and the thought brought an end to her restless pacing.

She went quickly up to her room, stood there, looked round, no change. And taking especial notice of its simple contents. One small iron bed, a table and chair, and in the corner a small chest of drawers, on which stood a small mirror which, for no reason at all, she suddenly bent to, seeing nothing, for the room was getting dark. An abruptly lifted latch sent her flying downstairs, and she opened the door to her neighbour.

'Mari! Glad you came. Come and sit here. Mervyn's just

gone; how lucky it was his meeting Mr Ellis. He's going to collect my sister at the station and bring her over here. That is a relief.'

'Yes, he expects her to get here some time after nine,' Mari said. 'Mervyn and I have been wondering what you'll do now?' she added.

'Do. Me? I'll stay on here of course – it's my home, I'll manage.'

'You missed your chance, dear, but your sister seized hers. Not many would have done what you did, leaving that nice teaching job in Manchester, coming here.'

'What else could I do?'

'Difficult, I know.'

'I couldn't leave Father on his own, could I? My mind was quite made up on that.'

'I admire your forgiving nature, dear, but your father's gone now. I wish something nice would happen for you, Cadi.'

When Cadi burst out laughing, it gave her visitor much pleasure. 'The times you've teased me about that,' said Cadi, and went off to make tea.

Sharing it, Cadi asked her if she had come on the bicycle.

'Yes, and I must now get back, dear. I'm sure your sister and Mr Ellis will be here any moment now.'

'I little thought,' said Cadi, 'that last Sunday would be our last walk.' But Mari said nothing, and she understood.

'*I must* go now, dear,' said Mari, and Cadi heard it, but did not move, and seemed not to hear the opening and closing of the door. She was thinking of Mr Ellis, who would soon arrive with her sister, Lucy. And for a moment or two the former obliterated the latter, for she now seemed no longer in the

13

kitchen, but walking a mountain road with her father, on those Sundays when, flanked by him, and Mervyn Edwards of Y Ffridd, they made their way with others, in all weathers, and came to the big, high door that was already open and inviting, and entering and taking the same bench as they always had. So now, Mari had gone, but the chapel was in the kitchen, and she saw it all anew. She was sat beside her father, listening to Guto Ellis proclaiming upon the things that were real, and those that were not. And she saw him now, hunched and stiff in his seat, who, with others, stared into eternity. Sunday was closeness for them both, but always her own most conscious moment was pinned to ground. And after Mr Ellis had spoken, the voices broke upon air, and everybody sang, the singing rising and falling, and seeping out through the partly open door onto a mountain road. And an awaited moment when Mr Ellis closed his eyes, and bent together heads seemed closer still. She listening to her father's heavy breathing, hoped all was well. Her worry about his health was a very private thing which she discussed with nobody. So came the final voices upon the air, and the last words from Mr Ellis, after which all rose to their feet and stepped out to end up as various knots upon the road. Groups broke into conversation, often about the weather, but always about what was root to them. Sometimes their absorption was so great that they would fail to notice the minister rise and emerge, closing the big doors after him. Only the sudden spitting from an ancient Austin signalled to them that at this moment the world was real. Gradually they broke up and departed, in groups, and sometimes alone, to wend their ways home under a wide sky. And Cadi would walk back to Pen y Parc, and say goodbye to the 'sheep' man from Y Ffridd.

I shan't go tomorrow, she told herself. And once I used to look forward to it, and always enjoyed the walk with them. I wish Mari had stayed; it'll be strange seeing Lucy after all this time. She ran to the window when she heard the sound of a car pulling up in the lane, and she threw open the door to see the tall Mr Ellis, preceded by a woman coming quickly up the path. They reached the door, and he was the first to speak.

'Here we are, Mrs Stevens,' he said.

'It was good of you, Mr Ellis,' Cadi said. 'Thank you.'

'Tut tut,' replied Mr Ellis with a wide sweep of the hand, and Cadi followed him to the door.

'Very sorry about your father,' he said, and she felt his hand on her own.

'I'm obliged to you,' she said, suddenly followed by her sister, who in turn thanked him profusely for his kindness.

'Cadi!'

'*Lucy!*'

And they embraced, and held each other for a moment or two, after which Cadi fussed, helping her off with her out-door things, bringing in the single suitcase stood on the step outside.

'Do come and sit down,' said Cadi. 'You look well.'

'I am well, dear, and what about you?'

'Me?'

'You, dear.'

They might never have been born in the same house, breathed similar air, had the same parents. The two sisters now sat opposite each other at the kitchen table. Though they were of almost equal height, the contrast between them was striking. Lucy was heavily built, rosy cheeked, full-bosomed, whose every movement emphasized her physical content, whereas Cadi was tall and slim, and her attractive features would stand out from others in a landscape, and her movements were graceful. Sat thus, they stared at each other as would strangers on initial confrontation. In this moment a curious shyness lay between them, and an awareness of it, but their thoughts were different. Just looking at her sister, Cadi seemed to multiply the years of absence, but Lucy's mind contained only one single day, this, and her abrupt arrival after long absence, after a long, boring journey by two trains, to the house where everything was still, and a father silent.

'I'll go up,' said Lucy, and went up, and Cadi followed her slow climb of stairs, and thought, she looks comfortable, but then she always did.

And each in turn could travel back years, and in their ears catch the echoes of what had seemed to them a continuously sounding anvil, when, stood together at the door of the forge they would look up to see their father towering, see the sparks fly, and in due time hear the expected explosion, as the huge beast, now shod, bounded forth as from the bars of a cage.

Her hands folded, and leaning on the table, Cadi heard the movements upstairs, and the sudden exclamation of her sister.

'Oh, Father!'

She crossed to the stairs and called up, 'I'm making tea, Lucy,' but there was no reply, but later she joined Cadi in the back part of the house.

'It's sad,' said Lucy, and a handkerchief out, and 'He has changed. What happened?'

'Out staking a mile away and a rotten branch fell on him. I had to go out and find him. But I did, and I carried him back here. It was all over in four days, pneumonia.'

'*Carried* him?'

'That's right. Will you take the kettle and the pot,' said Cadi, and they returned to the kitchen. And again they sat opposite.

'It's sad,' cried Lucy, but Cadi said nothing, and served her tea.

'I'll make supper soon,' said Cadi, then, slowly sipping at her tea, she studied this visitor from behind the mountain, and in great detail, noting everything Lucy wore, and bending closer, began fingering the material of her two-piece suit, the hat, the gloves, now removed and lying on a corner table. Yes, Lucy did look well, she thought, the one that got away.

'Cadi?'

'Yes?'

'What will you do now, dear?'

And Cadi thought instantly, dear, well well.

'What d'you think I'll do, Lucy?'

'You can't stay here on your own, dear.'

'I can.'

'You will?'

'It's my home, and I've always, well I seem to have been here for ages,' but Lucy thought that the smile was very forced.

'*Really?*'

'It's what I said, dear,' and abruptly, after a short pause, 'How's your husband, Lucy?'

And it brought a smile at once, and a little excited, Lucy leaned over.

'David, his name's David, I thought you knew that, dear.'

'I didn't.'

'I'm glad I came, dear, and even though I hardly ever wrote, I did always think of you, and wondered about you, here, alone with Father.'

'Tell me about him,' Cadi said.

'Who?'

'Your *husband*.'

The tone suddenly changed, and the voice was gentle.

'You'd like David, dear; such a good man, so thoughtful, and I still thank God for the day I met him. He said he'd try to come over, but I'm not so sure; it means him finding a replacement at the Post Office at short notice, still, I hope he'll try. Everything here seems strange to me, Cadi.'

'Yes, it would do, dear, but it's my home.'

'Sometimes, I feel I'll never forgive myself over that affair, yes,' and suddenly Cadi's hand was clasped in her own. 'The way you had to come here, of all places; I cursed the day I saw it for the first time.'

'I'd rather not talk about it,' Cadi said. 'More tea?'

'Thank you,' replied Lucy, whose tone of voice was now more direct, with a certain stiffness of utterance.

'There's so much I want to talk about, Cadi,' Lucy said, and again Cadi said nothing. 'I wonder if Father left anything, dear?' And it seemed to Lucy that she would have to call her sister back, as from a great distance, when she added, sharply, 'Didn't you hear what I said?'

'I did. And I hadn't forgotten. The whole history of this house lies in that big tea canister over your head. I'll empty it out later on.'

And Lucy mused. Why hadn't Cadi married, so attractive.

18

Must have met somebody. And she was so silent, and with some questions showed an air of indifference. After which reflection she delivered the ultimatum.

'When will it be, dear?' she asked.

'Monday, I hope, which reminds me I must go off and see Mr Hughes of Y Fraich first thing in the morning...'

'Mr Hughes?' said Lucy, groping, finishing her tea, banging down the cup.

'The undertaker,' Cadi said.

'Oh. I see.'

'We're rather scattered in these parts,' Cadi announced, and was quickly interrupted by her sister, who exclaimed, rather raspishly:

'Don't tell me *that*,' but Cadi appeared not to have heard the remark.

'Who is Mr Edwards?'

'Farm higher up. He's sheep.'

'Oh!'

'I'll make supper.'

'Why yes, of course,' replied Lucy, and got up to follow Cadi into the back, but her sister swung round, saying, 'You sit down, get warm, and you look tired after your journey. I can manage.'

Later, Lucy watched the supper being prepared, with Cadi bent over the fire, frying pan in hand, in which lay two slices of bacon, and one egg.

'Would you lay the table?'

'Certainly,' and Lucy was busy in a moment.

'There,' said Cadi. 'Sit down and have it.'

'What about you?' asked Lucy, watching Cadi cut one large round of bread, and butter it, which she put on her plate.

19

'Is *that* all?'

'In these parts,' said Cadi, 'we don't fuss'; after which she poured out the tea.

Lucy cried: 'Cream! Well well! Don't see much of that our way.'

'Drink it up,' said Cadi, and again remarked on how tired she looked. It brought a sigh from Lucy, and 'That awful station!' she replied. Cadi watched. How delicately her sister removed the fat from the bacon, nibbled at her supper. Then suddenly, she looked up.

'Poor Father,' she said.

It raised no response in Cadi, who thought only of the occasions when her sister might have remembered her father was living in Wales, on a holding known as Pen y Parc. How curt she had been with her neighbour, Mari. Still full of her long journey, she supposed.

It made her think of Averton, that man named Stevens. Lucy, pushing away her plate, a supper scarcely eaten, now contemplated her sister.

'It's hard to believe, Cadi,' she said quietly.

And Cadi snapped back, 'But it's true.'

Lucy coughed clear an instant feeling of embarrassment, saying, 'You haven't changed much, Cadi, and you look well.'

'I...' began Cadi, but Lucy again interrupted.

'The least I expected when I arrived was that the doctor would be here. And your telegram seemed rather late to both of us, dear.'

'He'll be here when he can; he has a big round to do, but you wouldn't know that,' replied Cadi in icy tones, and got up to clear the table, on which Lucy, too, got up.

20

'Don't bother. You sit quiet there. You've had a long journey,' and went off and left her sister alone by the fire.

Lucy stared into the flames, twiddled her fingers, heard the sound of washing-up out in the back, and mused again. Hasn't forgiven me, really; nobody's forgiven me, just because I was determined to make my own life. And here I am now, back in this wilderness.

In the back, Cadi talked to Cadi. Only came because she *had* to, rather a nuisance that Father died. She stood at the sink, hand on the running tap, which for some reason she allowed to go on running, and even wondered why. Then Lucy called. 'Cadi!'

They were close again, looking, searching each other, waiting.

'There's lots of things I'm sorry about,' Lucy said.

'So am I.'

Lucy, trying to smile, smiling, took her sister's hand, and then the gentle voice, the hint. 'Won't you tell me about yourself, dear?'

'What's to tell?'

'You know what I mean.'

'I don't know what you mean, Lucy,' Cadi replied, and suddenly added, 'We go to bed early in these parts.'

'I can take a hint.'

'I didn't mean that.'

'What did you mean?'

'I've been making another kind of journey myself,' said Cadi, 'and I feel just as tired as you do,'

'I *am* sorry.'

'Perhaps we'd better retire,' said Lucy. 'Perhaps we'll both feel different after a good night's sleep.'

'We mustn't start quarrelling, dear.'

'Of course not.'

'Where's my case, Cadi?'

'I took it up.'

'Where'll you sleep?'

'I'll manage,' said Cadi.

'You appear to be very good at managing,' snapped Lucy, and followed her sister to the stairs, paused a moment, and then a rush of words, 'you're quite right, we'll feel better in the morning. And we mustn't start quarrelling.'

'I'm afraid you didn't much enjoy your supper,' said Cadi.

They stood outside the door of the small room, then Cadi kicked it open, saying, 'You know the way, dear.'

A curious feeling came over Lucy as she sat down on the edge of the bed, watched her sister light first the candle and later a lamp.

'I know this room better than you,' remarked Lucy. 'I know it inside out.'

'Just fancy that.'

Cadi drew the curtains, but did not close the window.

'There! And, oh, the stove, of course. I know you always hated the cold, dear.'

'Thank you,' replied Lucy, and began a minute inspection of the room's entire contents. No change whatever, not a thing altered. Extraordinary all that time away. Of course I know how she feels, I know how *I* feel, too, and I'll be glad when it's all over, and repeated to herself, all *over*.

Cadi sat down.

'Nothing's changed here, Cadi.'

'I've changed,' was the prompt reply.

With the greatest of effort Lucy produced a smile, saying, 'Mustn't forget what we said a moment ago, dear.'

'I'll remember.'

'I must go and light that stove,' Cadi said, but did not move.

'Perhaps you'd best do it now then.'

The moment Cadi left the room, Lucy got up, wandered slowly around, then suddenly turned to the bed, and pulled down the sheets, but the moment she heard the feet on the stairs she hastily turned them back again, as Cadi bounced in, and put the stove in a corner furthest from the door.

'Would you like a glass of hot milk, dear, help you sleep?'

'No. I'm sure I'll be well away the moment my head touches that pillow. I cursed both those trains today, dear, so *slow.*'

Standing near the door, Cadi asked herself if there was really anything more to say.

'And do sit down, Cadi,' said Lucy, and pulled her back to the bed.

'That's right. Let me have a good look at you. What an age it seems, and you've hardly said a word since I arrived.'

'We can talk tomorrow.'

'We must talk about plans, dear.'

'*Plans?*'

'Naturally, David and I are wondering what you'll do now. I do hope he can manage it.'

'How is your husband?'

'David, dear *David.* He's well, thank God. You know the more I think about that man, the more I realize how much I depend on him. He's so *thoughtful,* considerate, helpful. There's a Mr Penfold that might help. In which case David'll come in the car...'

'*Car?*'

'Only a little one, dear. Actually if we'd both been free we would have booked into a hotel somewhere; it is rather cramped here.'

It made Cadi burst out laughing. 'Forty-odd miles away,' she said. 'Sure you won't have that hot milk, Lucy. Wish you would. And now I'll leave you to your beauty sleep. And it was good of you to come all that way, Lucy, it really was.'

'He's my *father*,' protested Lucy, stung by her sister's remark.

'And mine, too. Try to remember, won't you.'

'We're quarrelling again.'

'Damn! Sorry, Lucy.'

'Forget it.'

'Goodnight,' said Cadi, and rushed out, banging the door behind her.

Lucy got up and stood behind the door, heard her sister go down, and the first step in the echoing kitchen. She then undressed and got into bed, blew out the lamp, and settled herself down with a feeling of relief. How strange to be here, after years, and at such a sad time. She thought of David, and hoped he would come, and soon. Lying stretched in the too small bed, one long arm hanging over the side of it, she suddenly imagined that the room was beginning to close about her, holding her in.

The day I got out of this room, I saved myself.

Only then did she realize that the window was open, and she got up and shut out the wind, and the irritating sound of a branch scratching against glass. And then she felt a rising heat, a strong smell in the room, and remembered the stove. Immediately she got up and blew it out, and then settled herself again. Lying in the darkness she became aware of a weight greater than that of the blankets that covered her, and at once closed her mind to it, since it might have involved a long, inner journey, and for the present the memory of a long, dreary one from Averton seemed more than sufficient. Thoughts crept up on her which she was in no mind to pursue. Then suddenly Cadi was real, almost seemed to be in the room with her, sat by this bed, and completely silent.

She has changed, almost like meeting another stranger, really, and in a flash was back in the moment of embarrassment, and, without knowing why, suddenly covered her head with the sheet, as though to blot this knowledge out.

If only she'd married, still attractive. I watched her this evening, and even wondered if she was conscious of it. No, perhaps not; perhaps she was indifferent to it, didn't care. Poor Cadi.

These thoughts induced a restlessness, even against her very will, since she simply longed to sleep, forget the whole disturbing day. Speaking aloud beneath the sheets, she could not hide a certain grudge in her own voice. 'She was always more clever than I was. *And* she got away from here then, more than I did, and Father was so gone on my marrying that Evan Pugh. Thank God I escaped that, the last thing I was determined to do was marry a farmer.'

Suddenly she sat up in the bed, was more aware of the silent house. Here I am, *back,* and I do feel ashamed of something, something; wish I could pin it down. Yes, I did ignore her, and I don't know why. Wish I could just fall asleep, sleep the whole night through. Yes, I suppose I did think of myself, and she lay down again, stared into the darkness.

How *old* Father looked. God, I wish I'd never written him that letter. And he never replied to it. I remember that, it was like being struck. Yes, Cadi did write me two years ago to tell me Father was ill. And I never answered that, either. Sitting talking to her down there this evening, she even asked me why. I felt terrible, but then I said it to her, straight. I was afraid to come over, I'd the awful feeling that if I turned up, I'd *never* get back.

It brought David back, very close; she could feel him there and she wished he'd come. I do hope that Mr Penfold will be kind, and take over for him. I feel absolutely lonely in this house. God! I always hated it.

She turned over on her side, face to the wall; she ran a hand over this, got the feel of it. She turned over on her back, pressed her fingers to her forehead.

I had to come.

She did not know why she so abruptly left the bed, and crossed to the window, which she now opened, and let the wind rush in. And she remained stood there, looking out on a great bank of darkness, then as suddenly shut it again. Should she light the lamp?

She lit it, and then walked to the small bookcase on the wall, stared at what she saw there. Some books. Back in Averton there were none, save copies of the big encyclopedia that David was fond of dipping into. 'I was never one for books, *really*, no,' and the moment she said it Averton came alive, with its comforts, a warmth, a contentment, and all those marvellous magazines that David gets for me because he knows that's what I like best, and even saw herself in the snug sitting-room, sat on the floor, surrounded entirely by a shoal of women's magazines, of every size and colour, and this was Lucy's real world. And she stared on at the books, tentatively pulled one out, sat down on the bed, and studied the title under the lamplight. *Twm o'r Nant*, she read. Oh!

She hadn't heard of him. But Cadi had.

Yes, she was cleverer than me; how lucky she was to get away to Manchester that time, teaching children. Silly woman, really, ever coming to this dump. No, no, I mustn't say that. And *why* did Father pull up his roots like that, so sudden, seemed no reason for it. I'll never understand why. She thought of life back in the Ty Coch days. The stern house. She thought of her mother, willing slave, she thought of the forge. Perhaps it wasn't paying, after all, perhaps there was a reason for the move, and she thought of *his* father, hardworking, stolid. He had built it up, made something of it, expected his son to carry it on. The monotony of days there, with nothing happening. Like father, like son, no change; what's there *is there*, accept it, say nothing, work. Yes, they both of them worked hard. And so did we. Mother, Cadi, me, just servants there; it might have gone on forever. The looks we got, the hints that were thrown at us, do what everybody does, marry a farmer. Poor Cadi doesn't even know how lucky she was. I wish she'd throw it all up, come back with us to Averton, find some new interest and she might even meet some nice man. What was there *here?* Nothing. Yes, she must talk to her tomorrow. If only she could sleep, but crowded thoughts would not disperse, and she turned and turned in the uncomfortable bed. Again she got up, tiptoed to the door, quietly opened it, listened. Not a sound. And Cadi. Where was she? Somewhere down there, sleeping?

'I'll manage,' she said, and the way she said it to me. I've a good mind to go down now, and see where she *is* sleeping. This house seems even smaller than it was, miles away from anywhere, from people, from everything. Suddenly she opened wide the door, crept out onto the landing, listened again. Silence. Quietly, she closed the door, and got back into bed.

Wish I'd brought some aspirins with me. Wish David would *come*. It's all so strange to me, being here again; little did I think I'd be here twenty-four hours ago. I must have a good look round in the morning. She hasn't said a word about the place, shown me nothing. I *never* saw hands like it, so worn, old looking. There's something she has to tell me, God, I wish she'd talk, be more open, her manner almost frightened me, and she seems so casual about everything. I wonder if she *cried*.

And at last sleep found her, so that she did not hear her sister coming upstairs, nor the door of that other room open and close, as she entered it carrying two blankets over her arm. Later, Lucy's quiet breathing turned to snores.

2

Cadi lay flat upon the floor, in the dead room, one blanket under, and one over her, and close to her ear the fast tick of the little clock she had brought with her the only sound in the room, as she lay pondering about things, the long day, the shock of yesterday, the curious feeling she had of being alone, being free, and afraid of it. The strangeness of things. And she, too, like Lucy, lay there and listened to the wind. Her thoughts were of stairs, and a sudden loud creak in them as her father would make his ascent, and she heard also the peculiar thud as his bedroom door closed. This thud had seemed to echo through the whole house. She thought of her room, and the woman in it, and remembered that at the end of her own day she would lie close to the lamp, and read the papers that told her of a world beyond the mountain. Then, she would settle herself for the night, ever aware of the desert that lay between her father's room, and her own.

I never thought Lucy would come.

She thought of days good and bad, and one that was black came clear, a day that was nailed to the ground in a moment of hot anger, remembered the woman's name, so innocently spoken, after which the silence she accepted, an edict of the dumb.

Poor Lucy hasn't a clue.

She lay close to the wall, but she did not sleep. At a fixed hour a tiny bell would ring, and she would leave this room, and go down into another day.

I hope she's comfortable and sleeps well. How big she is, how strong. Not like me. And *beaming* with good health.

The blankets fell away from her, and she sat up to listen, thinking she had heard a movement in the next room, but there was nothing to listen to save the tick of the clock, and it seemed to her the only real thing in the room. Feeling stiff, she got up and crossed to the window, and stood there, looking out, and there was nothing to see but the darkness beyond it. She wrapped the blanket tighter about her shoulders. Staring out at nothing.

I can't believe it's happened.

The darkness seemed to vanish with a mere closing and opening of the eyes, and there before her lay the green fields, and she saw moving across them two close together men, their heads slightly bent, as they went forward to deal with the last of the first hay. So, rooted at this window, she was looking into another day and another time, and watching men walk on, closest to all they knew, was real, and would never end.

'Poor Father,' Cadi said, and crossed the room and lay down again, and was suddenly glad that she had banked up

30

the fire downstairs. Lying there, the days wound themselves about her, and she wished for the night to go. And she thought of life that was simple at Pen y Parc, where her father grew inwards, and she remembered the world beyond it, and found herself imprisoned by questions and by answers.

Why am I here? Because you couldn't do anything else. I was sorry for him, and that was the bond. I once wrote Lucy and told her Father was far from well and would she come?

So the lines in a letter from Lucy came clear, pressing, insistent, and she spoke them to herself. 'I can't come, and I'm sorry about it. I only remember going away. No. I daren't come; I might never get back.'

It brought close the moment when she had read it to her father, and remembered the look in his eyes, and the blank face.

He was ill, but I had to tell him. She wouldn't come, and he said nothing, nothing.

She stirred under the blanket.

So I came, and here I am. Lived with him, worked with him, listened to him, said yes, obeyed him, and was sometimes afraid of him, and always sorry.

So at last she gave way, pressed her face into the blanket, cried.

She awoke feeling cold, wondering how long she had been asleep, got up, folded the blankets, placed the little clock inside one shoe, then crept quietly to the door, and went out. It seemed even colder on the small landing. She stood there, shoes in hand, listened for a moment, then went down to the kitchen. She put away the blankets, stirred the fire, and flung

31

some dry sticks to it, and she was glad it was still warm. When the fire brightened she went out and half filled a kettle, put it on, waited for it to boil. And it was still strange to be sitting there alone, and never again would she listen to known footsteps. The clock told her it was a quarter to five. After making tea, she flung a small log to the fire. There was a feeling of satisfaction as she slowly sipped the hot tea. Tomorrow was already here, and there were things to be done. It made her think of Monday. Yes, it must be Monday. After breakfast she would leave Lucy to herself, and get off to make the arrangements with Mr Hughes. Perhaps Dr Morgan has already called at Y Fraidl, she thought. A charred stick fell to the hearth, and sounded like thunder.

She talked about plans. What plans? How silly. She would remain here; it was the only place to be, and it had root, meaning. She thought of Averton, that faraway place. What on earth would she do there?

It made her think of Lucy's husband, whom she had never met. Would he come? She doubted that. The name Pen y Parc had long since vanished beneath the Averton waves.

No. I'll carry on, doing the same things every day, and she thought of the simplicity of it all.

Glad Miss Jones the Missions won't be coming until Wednesday, perhaps Thursday. It would be all over by then. The thought of Miss Jones brought a faint smile, remembering her last visit, having tea together, and listening to the latest news that she brought with her. What an admirable person she was, tramping about like that in all weathers, collecting money to save all those dark souls away in Africa. And Cadi supposed it was somewhere at the end of the world.

32

She thought of her neighbours, the Edwardses. Real friends, and how good they'd been these last few days, and remembered an occasional supper with them, listening to the radio, playing cards together, and always watching the clock, and the message it sprung for her at a vital moment. Ten o'clock, and back to Pen y Parc, and she always knew the length of the leash.

Lying well back in the chair, she wandered in such moments, the half empty mug now dangling in her hand. Then, and almost without realizing it, she closed her eyes for a moment or two. The mug went slack in her hand, and the liquid sprayed both skirt and hearth. Only when it fell and smashed at her feet, was she aware that she was falling asleep.

Oh God! I'm sure I've woken her up, and she crept to the foot of the stairs, and listened.

The grandfather clock struck the hour, and made her jump.

Was that something moving upstairs. Was she awake, wasn't she? But nothing moved; no voice called. And then she heard it. 'She is awake,' she exclaimed under her breath, and then wished she was not. Back to the stairs again, calling softly, and at the same time suddenly wishing that she was miles from the place.

'Are you awake?'

The reply was immediate, and it was leaden. Yes, she was awake, and had been for some time. And what was the time?

'Are you *there*, Cadi?'

'Yes.'

And louder. 'Are you down there, Cadi?'

Cadi regretted the shout the moment she made it. 'I'm here, I'm *always* here.'

An instant silence, and then the voice that was casual. 'I'll bring you up a cup of tea,' Cadi said.

'I'll come down.'

'And I said I'll bring it up.'

When she entered with the small tray she found her sister standing at the window in her dressing-gown, and she heard the door open, but did not move. Erect and stiff, she stared through glass; saw nothing beyond it.

'Do come and sit down, the tea's nice and hot, dear.'

They sat on the bed together.

'I hope you had a good night, Lucy?'

'I was all right. And you? Where did you sleep?'

'In the kitchen.'

Lucy was glad of the tea, the warm feeling of a mug between her hands.

'I'll be going out after breakfast,' Cadi said.

'Where?'

'To see Mr Hughes.'

'Who's he?'

'The undertaker, the only one for miles.'

'Oh – yes... I see. The tea's lovely, dear.'

'I'm glad.'

'I'd best get dressed,' said Lucy, and handed her sister the mug.

'No need to come down yet. Nothing to do down there.'

'What is the time?'

'A quarter to six.'

'*What?*'

34

'Ten to, to be exact,' Cadi said.

'Oh *no* – is that all?'

'That's all. More tea?'

There was no reply, and she watched her sister begin to dress, thought of her feet lying beyond the too small bed. Perhaps she'd had an uncomfortable time of it. Dressed, Lucy went back to the window.

'Nothing to see out *there*,' said Cadi, and half rose from the bed, as Lucy came back with the whiplash reply, 'There never was.'

She crossed to Cadi, made to smile, and didn't, then asked if there was a fire 'down there'.

'There's always a fire,' replied Cadi, 'and all you can do if you come down is sit by it.'

'I do hope David turns up today.'

'I wonder,' said Cadi, and walked to the door.

'I think you'd like him, dear.'

Cadi turned round. 'You haven't had a very good night, have you? I'm sorry.'

'I'm sure you are,' snapped Lucy, and joined her at the door.

'We're not going to quarrel, I hope.'

'Of course not; we mustn't. Yes, I was awake half the night. When I look back, think of Father coming to *this* place... mad – that's what I say.'

'Are you coming down?'

'Of course I'm coming down,' replied Lucy, and preceded her sister into the kitchen. 'Ah! Warmer here, anyway.'

'I gave you the stove, dear.'

'I blew it out; awful smell.'

Lucy sat close to the fire, twiddled her fingers and looked round.

35

'Used to think Pen y Parc tiny,' said Lucy, 'and looking at it now, it seems to have grown even tinier, dear.'

'I'd ceased to notice,' said Cadi. 'One gets used to a thing after a while, and not minding about it sometimes helps.'

'Cadi.'

'Yes?'

'Odd the doctor hasn't called, dear, I even thought he might be here when I arrived.'

'He does have a rather big round, Lucy, don't worry about it, he'll turn up all right. What time d'you want breakfast?'

'Whenever you're having it, of course.'

'Which is now, since there are always things to be done in this place.'

'What?'

'What d'you think,' said Cadi, and vanished into the back.

I wish she'd settle, relax, sit down, *talk*. I know nothing. It was slowly growing light, and once more she went to the window. A little walk might freshen me up, she thought, and when Cadi came in she found her with her coat in her hand.

'Surely you're not going out,' said Cadi.

'I thought a walk round the house would freshen me up.'

'You'll want two coats as warm as that one,' replied Cadi, and began setting the table. 'Since you dislike the bacon, I'm giving you two eggs. All right?'

'Yes, dear. Very nice. I did enjoy that first cup of tea.'

Cadi made no comment, and it seemed the sensible thing to do. The silly questions she asks, I'd like to explode. They sat in, ate.

'I don't know how you can live just on bread and butter,' Lucy said, but it brought only a quick smile from her sister. 'One gets used to things, and after a while hardly notices.'

36

'Sure you wouldn't like me to come with you to see Mr Hughes?'

'Not really, and I dislike the idea of nobody being here, and Father upstairs. I shan't be longer than I can help.'

'Very well. Have you thought any more about what I said, coming back to Averton for a few days?'

'No, Lucy, I haven't,' Cadi replied, and then exploded.

'How on earth can I do that, even if I wanted to? You don't expect me to walk out and leave the stock. Do you?'

'A short stay, what's that? Surely your nice neighbour wouldn't mind seeing to things for a day or two.'

'I wouldn't impose on them; they're too good, neighbours.'

'Suit yourself then.'

'*I must.*'

'I shan't mention it again,' said Lucy, and Cadi said nothing, but got up and collected her outdoor things.

'But it's only half past seven, dear.'

'I did notice. Would you mind clearing the table? Hope you enjoyed your breakfast.'

'I did. I feel better now. I *wish* we could have walked into the village together. All changed there now, I'm sure.'

'I'm going beyond the village. By the way, should anybody call, just tell them where I've gone, and that I shan't be long. One of the Edwardses might look in. And Dr Morgan may call this morning, too.'

'And I'll be glad to see him,' announced Lucy. 'At the moment everything seems so odd to me, Cadi, and this business, so *sudden*.'

Cadi was stood at the window, Lucy hugging herself at the fire, and her sister swung round, saying, 'What? Dying of pneumonia. Father wasn't a young man, Lucy. Far from it.'

Lucy got up, joined Cadi at the window, and both stood there, looking out.

'It's very early, dear,' said Lucy.

'This isn't Averton,' replied Cadi.

'Don't be like that, Cadi. Of course I know how you feel; of course I understand, but why be so short with me?'; thinking: why so early; what's the hurry. Yes, why not later, one of the Edwardses might drop in, we could go together, I don't want to be left here on my own. And abruptly, anxiously, 'Couldn't you go later, dear? I'd love to come with you, really I would.'

'What are you frightened of, Father? *Now?* I'll only be away about an hour, dear. Heavens! You look quite upset. I must show you round when I come back.'

Lucy said nothing – there seemed nothing to say, and her sister's hand was already restless on the door knob.

'Keep a nice fire, dear,' Cadi said, opened the door, and left the house.

The moment the door closed a strange feeling came over Lucy, and she stiffened in the chair. She felt as though she had emerged as from some dreamlike state, and it seemed to her, too, that for the first time she was getting the real feel of the house, the damp, and the silence. She jumped to her feet and rushed to the door, stopped dead, stared at it, as though expecting a knock, willing it, from somebody, from anybody.

I hope she won't be long, I don't like being here on my own, and she began a slow pacing of the kitchen, up and down and up and down, propelled to this action, as though the very act of walking might in some way help wash away

38

this strange, unexpected upsurge of feeling, as she muttered to herself, again and again, 'I wish she hadn't gone, left me here, I do hope she won't be long; I wish *somebody* would knock on that door. *Wish* I'd gone with her, wish she was *here*,' and thought of her husband. David. If *only* he was here now. What a lifebelt that would be. She stopped pacing, stood at the foot of the stairs, a finger pawing her lips, one hand gripping the banister, and then she went slowly up, and at the top of the stairs, stood again, looking round, looking down. The very sight of the two closed doors heightened her awareness of the situation. By some effort of will she managed to open the first door, peep in, enter. And he was still there. Hastily she covered his face, and then began a slow inspection of everything in the room, the known objects, Ty Coch drawing nearer and nearer, another time, the old days. She stood at a chest of drawers, on which stood a small oval mirror, but she did not look into it, her eyes cast down, staring at the three big drawers, and without any hesitation she opened the top one, and looked inside, only to hastily shut it.

I wish she hadn't left me like this. What on earth am I doing here, in this room?

Kneeling, she made a violent movement, and pulled out the bottom drawer, bent down, and looked at its contents. Why am I doing this? Her hand roamed about in the drawer, but she took nothing out, then suddenly looked up at the ceiling. There was something trance-like in these actions.

If David knocked now, how different everything would be.

She closed the drawer so violently that the mirror toppled, but she caught it as it came down, and this action made her turn sharply and look towards the bed, as though

39

an eye might open, watch her. She tiptoed out, went into the other room where she had spent her long night. And the ritual continued. Everything was examined anew, objects picked up and put down again, sometimes warily, sometimes adventurously, in the known place, the cell, the prison.

'When I think about it all,' she said.

She rushed headlong to the stairs, and down, back to the chair, the fire, and waiting, waiting.

Wish she'd *come*. Will that doctor call? If only somebody would *knock*.

The walls of the kitchen appeared to narrow about her, the ceiling itself to lower. Unable to hold back her feelings any longer, she left the house, stood for a moment in the path, then began a slow, leisurely walk round. No change. She paused at the big kitchen garden. I helped make that.

A glance in a byre, and the breath of three cows.

Had nothing when I left here.

And nearby, the sudden grunting of a pig. Nor that, either.

She stared across at three small fields, at the sour, wintry grass. And she supposed that something had come out of them. Hay perhaps. She ambled slowly down the path, leaned heavily against the little white gate. The light was coming in fast. She looked up at the sky. What an awful feeling that was, she told herself, suddenly gripped the gate, looked beyond it, longed for her sister's return, listened for steps in the lane. Then she went back and resumed her waiting, her mind full of Cadi as she stirred the fire, and replenished it, and she wanted her now, this very minute, but Cadi was walking elsewhere.

40

Her mind was peopled with instant regrets. *Why* hadn't she asked Cadi to call at the Post Office. There *might* have been a message from David. He might even have phoned, perhaps there was a telegram lying there already, and she read it in an instant. 'Arriving this morning, love, David.' From time to time she lay well back in the chair, looked upwards, listened, and she knew full well that there was nothing to listen to. She got up and went into the back, and like the journey upstairs, began examining everything, after which she went into what Cadi called 'the cold room', and saw the milk.

She makes lovely butter. Perhaps I could take some back with me.

Leaning over the sink, running her fingers over the clouded glass of a tiny window.

God! I once actually lived in this place, many a time stood here, wondered why it happened. Poor Father. Not once did he explain to me; I often wondered what he paid for this place. So secretive, but then he always was, and for a moment she felt herself back at Ty Coch.

Nothing ever happened to me, nothing, until we came to this place.

Again she was drawn to the window, looking out, hoping.

Wonder how long she'll be? And why did she have to go off like that, at such an hour. I won't sit here any longer.

She put on her outdoor things, glanced up the stairs as she opened the door, then half ran down the path, left the gate swinging open behind her, and did not stop running until she had reached the deserted lane.

Meet her on the way back, can't explain it to her, she wouldn't understand. She has changed.

Cadi walked on at a steady pace, her mind centred on one single thing, fixing everything with Mr Hughes. Three people had already passed her by, and one said he was sorry to hear about it, and one on a bicycle, waved, crying, 'Morning, Cadi,' almost without noticing her, as though nothing had happened. And then she came in sight of the house. It stood on a hill, a semi-detached house, to the right of which there stood a large shed, from the door of which she saw the light, and hurried on. Reaching it, she stopped. She could hear the sound of movements within. And had she arrived a few minutes earlier, she would have seen the doctor's small car just pulling clear of the house, in the shed of which a short conversation had taken place.

'Morning, Hughes.'

And the one called coming quickly to the door.

'Oh! Morning, doctor. You're early.'

'Yes, Mrs Richards, Llys, had me out early.'

'I did hear,' said Hughes. 'Well then?'

'You heard?'

'Madog Evans, yes, I did.'

'Cadi'll be down this morning.'

'Pen y Parc, the stranger,' said Hughes, but the doctor made no reply.

'How's the family?'

'Well enough, doctor, thank you.'

'You don't hit the tops very often these days,' the doctor said.

'Not unless I have to, no.'

'Well, I'm off.'

'Morning, sir,' said Hughes, and stood there watching the car distance. He then vanished into the depths of his shed. Cadi peeped inside, then called.

'Who's that?'

'Miss Evans.'

'Why, yes,' and Hughes emerged. 'Morning, miss.'

'Good morning.'

'I heard. Sorry about it, pneumonia, wasn't it?'

'Yes.'

'Better come inside then,' he said, and she followed him in. 'Not much more than two cats can turn in this place,' said Hughes, and now stood against a rough-hewn desk, over which hung a bright calendar, and she watched his finger run slowly across it, and heard him mutter, 'February ninth, forty six.'

Their conversation now dropped to whispers.

'Right then, Miss Evans, around seven to eight this evening. All right?'

'That's all right, Mr Hughes,' she said.

'Well, good morning,' he replied, his eye following her as she went, a tall, thin woman, a little bent, and suddenly vanishing round a corner.

Walking quickly home, the last person she expected to see was Lucy hurrying towards her, who, on sighting her, increased her pace. Cadi stopped dead, and anger rose in her as her sister approached.

'I'm sorry, dear,' said Lucy. 'Something came over me, and I just *had* to come out, couldn't sit there on my own, awful feeling. I am sorry, is everything all right, dear?' and all in a single breath.

'I'm sorry you left him alone, and I did ask you,' said Cadi curtly.

'I *had* to.'

Cadi held back her feeling of disgust, outpaced her sister, and hurried on. To have left him like that, she thought. 'Cadi!'

But she did not answer.

'When is it?'

And the reply was flung. 'Monday.'

'Oh... I see.'

Cadi swung round, saying, 'I've already *told* you, and Mr Hughes will be here this evening.'

Overloading an explanation, Lucy said, 'I can't describe to you how awful I felt the very moment you'd gone,' and then more abrupt, 'And the doctor never turned up, either.'

'He will.'

'Don't be angry with me.'

'And don't tell me,' replied Cadi sharply. They reached the white gate, stood for a moment or two. 'I'm sick looking at this path, we never seem to be able to get tidying it,' and hurried down, Lucy following.

'I'll be glad when it's all over,' said Cadi, and this time, the silence was Lucy's.

The two women entered the house.

'No message then?'

'Message?'

'From your *husband*,' Cadi said.

'No. Nothing yet, but I've a strong feeling he'll turn up,' and her voice rising as she continued, 'and I simply can't think of David leaving me *here*,' and she encompassed the kitchen with a wild wave of the hand.

Cadi hung her coat. 'I expect you'll be glad to be out of it, Lucy.'

'I never said that,' protested Lucy, flinging her arms round her sister, who felt her shaking as she stuttered out, 'Please, dear. I know we're both worked up at present, don't let's quarrel.'

Cadi could only look at her in astonishment, for her eyes had moistened. She's not going to break down, surely, she thought, and freed herself from the embrace.

They sat opposite each other, and Cadi waited for the question she knew was coming.

'I've often wondered what Father paid for this place,' said Lucy, and whenever she mentioned the house it was abrupt and dismissive.

'I used to wonder myself,' replied Cadi, 'indeed it's only a few weeks ago that I found out.'

'Who told you. How much?'

'Mervyn Edwards told me.'

'Mr Edwards?'

'Yes.'

'A complete stranger, and not you?'

'Twm Pugh might have told him, he was here doing odd jobs about, even before I came. Suppose he told Mervyn, too.'

'How much?' asked Lucy.

'Four hundred and fifty pounds.'

'What? For this place?'

'You know how secretive he was.'

'Who, dear?'

'*Father*.'

'I shouldn't think he left much,' said Lucy.

'How would I know, I've had other things to occupy my mind, dear'.

'There's no hurry.'

'And I must think about a midday meal. What would you like, Lucy?'

'Not that bacon,' said Lucy. And they both laughed.

'How about a nice omelette, Lucy, lots of eggs.'

'That'll do,' Lucy said, and followed her sister out. 'If only I'd thought of it, dear, you might have called at the Post Office, there might have been a message, *something*,' visioning it again, the telegram reading, 'Arriving half past five, love, David'.

'Early yet,' said Cadi, 'and if he's coming, then he'll just *come*.'

The words fell like stones. 'I reckon so,' replied Lucy.

She was stood at the sink, looking out on the big garden, and recalling her first days in it. Yes, it had improved a lot, but when I *first* saw it... oh dear, and she looked at Cadi. 'D'you know I came in here one afternoon, must have been about a week after he landed me here, and I saw the strangest thing, dear.'

Cadi put down the tray. 'Oh! And what was that?'

'Father was looking out of this very window, standing very still, and he was crying.

'Crying?'

'Crying. I was so surprised I just stood there, dumb, couldn't say a word, I'd never seen him cry ever, and so *still*. I just tiptoed back to the kitchen. Never actually seen a man crying.'

'It's hard to believe,' replied Cadi.

'It was awful.'

'All ready now,' said Cadi, and they went out.

'You make your own bread then?'

'Always have.'

'Very nice,' said Lucy. 'D'you know you've never once talked about Manchester, dear.'

46

'Should I?'

'I was thinking of it last night, your leaving that nice job at the primary school. I admire what you did, dear.'

'What else could I do? He was quite alone here, and you were finished with him.'

'*Cadi*!' The knife and fork fell to the floor, with a loud clatter, and Lucy hastily pulled out a handkerchief. 'Don't Cadi, *please*.'

When Cadi looked up her sister's face was hidden behind the handkerchief, and she hated herself for what she had said.

'Forgive me, Lucy, it was a horrible thing to say. Anyhow, it's all over now, finished.'

The handkerchief came down, and Lucy blubbered it out, 'I suppose so,' she said, and then retrieved the cutlery and left the kitchen.

Her eyes were quite moist; I wish I hadn't said it.

The remainder of the meal was eaten in silence.

'I thought we might go out after we wash up, Lucy, have a look round, you haven't been out yet.'

Lucy, lying, replied that she had not.

'Then let's go.'

And Lucy was never more glad, changed in a moment, tired of sitting, tired of restrictive space, and, always with her, the thought of another night in that room. Outside, she stared up at the sky.

'That wind last night, Cadi.'

'I heard it. Come along, dear,' Cadi said. They stood in the kitchen garden.

'Father and I made this,' said Lucy. 'It really has come on, hasn't it?'

47

'I should think so, after fifteen years.'

'First thing I saw here was a fine crop of dockleaves,' said Lucy, and though admiring the success of it, how orderly everything was now, she did not express it to Cadi.

'This way,' Cadi said, and they were on their way to the shippon.

'Well!' exclaimed Lucy, and caught the warm breath of three standing cows. 'He did make a go of it, dear,' she said, but Cadi didn't appear to hear. She stroked the flanks of all three, saying, 'That's Miranda, that's Jane, and that's Olwen.'

'Just fancy.'

'It's those dears that's kept us going, really,' said Cadi, and realized at once that the warm, close odour was something that made Lucy want to go. 'One can't live just on a garden. Last year we lost a lovely little heifer calf.'

'What a shame.'

'I only remember the cloud of blood,' said Cadi. 'Let's go on.'

'The smell,' exclaimed Lucy, as they neared the solitary pig.

'It's just like a friend,' Cadi said, and *they* went on.

Together they leaned on the gate, looked across the three small fields.

'D'you know what I was thinking just now,' said Cadi, and she turned and looked closely at Lucy. 'I was thinking of the afternoon I first got here, and Father met me at the station. I can see him now, standing there, waiting, and when I came up to him he gave me such a fierce embrace, quite frightened me. He'd even hired a car to take us back. But once inside the house everything seemed to change, it was Father at Ty

Coch, it was Father bellowing on Sunday mornings, d'you remember them...'

'*Do I*... Yes, I remember, dear, such a strict man, a real disciplinarian.'

'Poor Mother, nothing but a servant all her life.'

'He thought all women were servants, dear,' replied Lucy. 'I always thought you were lucky to get away that time.'

'Perhaps I was, I don't know, but now, well, everything's different. I've changed. I'm anchored here, and yet I don't mind. Our lives were reduced to the utmost simplicity. And strange, too, but the harder I worked, the more absorbed I became in everything I did, the further away I seemed to get from myself. It was a curious feeling, and I couldn't explain it.'

They reached the end of the field, leaned on another gate.

'The last six months were rather worrying though, since Father had practically given up doing anything. One afternoon the doctor stopped me in the road and told me he'd seen Father wandering around on the mountain. Quite scared me. Mr Owen from Tybaen brought him home. God, I was worried.'

'Shall we go back, dear?' asked Lucy.

'All right. Just a pure accident he should go off staking that day, he always liked that, and I suppose but for that you wouldn't even be here.'

'Just imagine a man in his sixties, throwing up everything, coming to a place like this. I often wonder why.'

'I did myself, dear, and we'll never get the answer to that, will we?' They turned; they ambled home.

'Father did work hard, I'll grant him that,' said Cadi, '*and* he wasn't always up to it. He was up at exactly the same

49

time morning after morning, around half six, and I'd hear him go out, but where to, and what for I never found out. Nor did I have the slightest intention of asking him. Always prompt at his meals, and he never lost that habit of his of salting his bread, and he seemed to enjoy whatever I put before him. D'you know we've had nothing but bacon for a whole week when the weather was really bad, but he never complained. He used to take a little paper called *The Star,* and that was the one day in the week when he seemed to me to be peaceful, relaxed. I can see him now, sitting by the fire, reading it, and the pipe in his mouth. I'd leave him alone then, and go up to my room. There were times when I just enjoyed being there, shutting the door.'

'What a strange shutaway life, dear,' Lucy said, and thought, not without relief, at last she's talking.

'You can get used to anything,' Cadi said. Their pace suddenly slackened, as though instinctively they realized there was more to come.

And secretly, Lucy began to feel a kind of contentment creeping in, and was now glad that she'd come out, and she hoped there would be no more sharp exchanges.

'Cadi?'

And for some reason Cadi stopped in her tracks. 'What?'

'D'you remember that other habit Father had,' began Lucy, 'remember that top room at Ty Coch, and how last thing at night he'd quietly open the door and come in with the lamp, and hold it high and look down at us.'

'Well, really. How strange, Lucy, yes I do remember. One night you were fast asleep, but I wasn't, and he came in so *quietly*, see him now holding up the lamp, looking down at us both. I shut my eyes tight, the room so silent, and I hardly

50

realized he had gone, and the door was shut again. Fancy remembering a thing like that. And ever since that time I've had an absolute horror of anybody staring down at me when I was asleep; it was like being suddenly naked. It even happened here, Lucy.'

'No!'

'It did indeed, and it really scared me. For once I wasn't reading, and the lamp was still lit, and in a flash there he was in the room, stood very still, looking down at me. It so scared me that after that night I always locked the door.'

'You don't think... surely...'

'No, Lucy, I definitely don't. But thank God, it never happened again.'

The moment they came in sight of the house, Lucy was back on the treadmill. 'I do wish David would come,' she said.

'He will.'

Lucy said nothing, thinking, the casual way she throws it off.

'There's still *time*, dear,' said Cadi, her train of thought broken, and now even her encouragement seemed flat, meaningless. Perhaps she was sick of listening to the name David. Yes, and what was *he* like, this unknown, unseen man who had made her sister so happy?

'Don't worry,' Cadi said. 'Remember we are isolated here. I wish I'd mended the bicycle, but somehow I never seem to get round to it. I haven't yet got over the shock.'

'Little did I imagine twenty-four hours ago that I would be *here*.'

'Who ever knows what's round the corner.'

'True enough,' replied Lucy.

'Let's go in now.'

And they walked back to the house.

Lucy was back in her chair, hands clasped, and occasionally kneading her fingers, looking into the flames. She felt restless, she felt confused, her mind fixed on one thing, her husband, and he was close, and she was listening.

'If I can, Lu, I will, you know that. But you see the difficulties, don't you? One can't always get somebody at a moment's notice.' And heard her own reply. 'Last thing I expected to see this morning, dear.'

'These things just *happen*,' he had said.

'But you will try, David?'

'Of course I'll *try*.'

To her the clock's ticks sounded as heavy as feet. She looked round, saw Cadi seated at the table, and in front of her the big canister she had just taken from the mantelpiece, and she noticed the flat of one hand lying limply on the lid. The last thing *she* wanted to think about? *Papers.* Nothing would seem right until her husband arrived.

'*Lucy.*'

But Lucy was temporarily lost.

'*Lucy!*'

Lucy jumped. 'Oh,' she exclaimed. 'What is it?'

'I meant to show you this, dear,' said Cadi, and took from behind the big green vase a piece of paper. 'I found it in the tin,' she said.

'What?'

'Here, read it,' and she handed her the paper.

'*Take me back beyond Ty Coch, where my father lies.*'

The paper fell from Lucy's hands. '*There?*' she said.

And how sharp Cadi was, the way she answered her. 'Well, it isn't *here*,' and she had to hide the annoyance she felt.

'The last place I wanted to see,' Lucy said.

Cadi got up, stood over her. 'It's years ago, Lucy; who'd remember anyway, and what does it matter. Nothing matters except carrying out Father's wishes; it would be wrong *not* to.'

Lucy's head bowed in meek submission. 'Yes – of course, dear.'

She stared at the big tin, the vase, the tiny clock. 'What time is it Monday?' she asked.

'Ten o'clock prompt.'

'What?'

'It's a long way.'

'Don't tell me *that*.'

'Really, Lucy,' Cadi began, and then found herself unable to say another single word. Was her sister that selfish? 'And we must go through these papers, dear. I've other things to do.'

'Oh dear,' said Lucy, and joined her sister at the table.

'I wish I hadn't to bother with it at all,' said Cadi, and her tone of voice was not lost on Lucy.

'Very well, open it then.'

Cadi tossed the entire contents of the tin onto the table. 'There!'

'That's it?'

'That's *all*.'

They both leaned in, glanced at each other, and then surveyed the paper-strewn table.

'Did Father have a bank, dear?'

Cadi exploded in her face. 'Don't make me *laugh*, no he didn't, why?'

53

'Wish I'd never mentioned it,' said Lucy. Already Cadi's fingers were picking at the pile. 'I wish David would come.'

Damn her husband, thought Cadi, delivering the ultimatum. 'D'you want to go through them with me, or don't you? It's your affair as well as mine, and I do know how inconvenient certain things are for you, dear.'

'Really, Cadi...'

With a single sweep of the hands Cadi swept the scattered papers into a heap. 'Let's burn the damned lot,' she said.

'Of course you can't, what a stupid thing to say, dear.'

'*Well* then?'

'I,' began Lucy, but Cadi wasn't even listening, and Lucy wasn't even *there*, she'd forgotten her, as now, bent over the table, her fingers moved about amongst the odd collection of letters, opened and unopened, receipts, notes and coins.

'Cadi.'

She did not look up, and she did not answer, totally absorbed as she was, looking at letter after letter, separating notes from coins.

'Would you like to count this,' said Cadi, and then very abruptly, 'Oh, here's something, and I think it's yours, dear.'

She held it in the air, 'do take it,' and pushed it across the table.

Lucy picked it up, read it, and Cadi saw her hand tremble. 'Oh God! It's the one I wrote him the night I got away from this place. Have you read it?'

'Why should I? It's addressed to Father.'

'I wish I'd never seen the thing,' said Lucy, crushed it into a ball, and flung it into the fire.

'Forget it,' Cadi said, and once more occupied herself with what lay before her.

There was a sudden silence.

'It had to be done, Lucy,' said Cadi, encouragingly.

But she could not look at Cadi, and bent her head, and in a shaky voice said, 'What a lot a little happiness costs.' There was no answer.

'*How much?*'

'Oh yes, sorry, dear, there's ninety-one pounds and some coins,' and she held up the notes.

'I don't know why I'm doing this, really,' said Cadi, 'none of it is important now,' and again there was no comment from Lucy. 'We'll share it,' she said.

'What?'

'The *money.*'

'I don't want anything, dear, *nothing.*'

'I said we'd share it.'

'I feel so ashamed; I wish I was miles away.'

'It won't be long, dear,' replied Cadi.

Lucy looked up and her voice broke, 'Can't you see I'm sorry.'

Cadi was touched by this, and could only stare, for in that moment it seemed to her as though the years had leapt on Lucy, suddenly older, even sad. I wish I'd burnt that letter, she said to herself. Lucy left the table, went and stood at the window, but Cadi went on.

'Do help me,' Cadi cried out, and Lucy returned to the table.

'What about all the other things?' asked Lucy.

'Things?'

'Well his clothes...'

'I'll give them away to anybody that wants them. I did tell you that Mr Hughes will be here around seven to eight.'

'You did.'

'D'you want to go up before they arrive?' asked Cadi.

'Not now,' replied Lucy.

And Cadi sensed what was occupying her sister's mind. 'Why don't you come and sit down,' she said, 'and don't worry about it. He'll turn up, I know he will.'

'D'you think so, really?'

Got him on the brain, thought Cadi.

'I did tell you his name's David.'

'I haven't forgotten,' said Cadi, and went back to the table, sat down. She picked up papers in the most cursory way, let them fall from her hand. What a mess, why not burn the lot of it. Wish I'd never shown her that letter, stupid of me; she's thinking about it now, I'm sure. I'll never mention it again, never ask her why or what she wrote. She just did it; and she wondered where feeling was that day. There was a telegram clear in her eye, and she read it. *'Please come, Father'*. I thought and thought about it, and I came, and I didn't want to, was contented where I was, but I did, *had* to, and saw him real, grown older, alone in a strange place. 'I've come,' I said, and he was pleased, seeing him, trying to smile, trying to say thank you. And here I am.

She bent so low over the table that her hair swept it, sending papers to the floor, and gripping tight to the table edge she felt the very warmth of the wood, as she stared at the mass of papers scattered beneath her. She closed her eyes. The clock struck, but she did not hear it, nor notice the gradually darkening kitchen as the light began to go. And behind her, the big sister draping the chair. And the two women were stone-still, in their fixed worlds.

56

3

The big woman from Averton sat quietly in her chair, but her thoughts were elsewhere, as the eyes closed against the brightness of the fire. And gradually she felt herself drawn away from it, up the stairs, back to the room, back to the night before, and only the owl's cry told her where she was. In the same bed, and fitfully sleeping, in the darkness, wanting to light a candle, but she seemed to have sunk further into her bed, where she had tossed and turned, and knew that the hounds were still with her, for a journey backwards was not yet over. Thoughts imprisoned her, and one was dominant. A thought of morning, going downstairs, seeing Cadi there. And there was a feeling of guilt, still close, and it drowned her husband, and it drowned Averton.

I wonder what time it is?

She thought of her father in the next room.

Wonder if he said anything, if he mentioned me? She hasn't said a word, told me nothing.

And she saw herself sitting long ago in the kitchen below, and waiting for a night that seemed never to end, and a letter in her hand.

Stealing off like that, and it shocked her now, recalling vividly the strange occasion. Perhaps before he died, he had cursed her. She wished she knew the time; she hated the room, and everything in it, and was reminded of this when she heard heavy, ringing footsteps pass by the house.

What can I say? What can I do? How long have I been here? And that dream I had, awful. And where is she? Cadi, sleeping, but where? How she's changed.

She forced herself to light the candle, forced herself from the bed, put on her dressing-gown, and went to the window, and opened it. How sharp the air, and what was *that?* Intently listening. Quickly shutting it she ran back to the bed, longed for the sleep that would not come.

Never imagined I'd be back *here*. I *wish* David would come. But *I am* here.

Was that someone moving about downstairs? Oh God! I wish I had a *clock*.

She wished to get up, to rush downstairs, *now*, but found she could no longer make the effort, could not move. She sat up, she lay back again, she stretched, she turned over, her face to the wall, and as she moved, the hounds moved. The rack again, and travelling backwards, to the very beginning of her journey.

It was cold at the station, where the wind swept down five platforms and sent the debris flying. A train was empty, but she was in it, and she had quite forgotten to close the door. She knew why she was here, she remembered being wakened at the usual time by her husband, who stood at the bedside, cup of tea dutifully in hand.

I woke, I looked at him, and he wasn't smiling.

So she glimpsed him for a moment, his other hand, and in it the telegram.

'What is it, David?'

'A telegram, dear.'

'Oh dear! *A telegram.*'

'Just come,' he said, and she sat up and he gave it to her. The hand shook, but finally she opened it, and read aloud.

'*Father died this evening, pneumonia, Evans, Pen y Parc.*'

'Oh God!'

She covered her face with her hands, and he said gently, 'I *am* sorry.'

'I'll have to go, dear,' she said, and let the telegram fall from her hand.

'Do have your *tea*, dear. A shock, I know, but *do* drink your *tea.*'

He sat on the bed, twiddled his fingers, looked anxiously at his wife, thought of the suddenness, the surprise of it. 'You'll have to go, Lucy.'

'Of course I'll have to go, I *know* that,' she replied sharply.

'I'd come with you if I could.'

'Yes, yes, I know, dear, but you have your work to do.'

She sipped slowly at her tea, and he bent over her, dropped his voice. 'I'll see what can be done. If I could get a replacement, but it's so sudden. I'll try, and if I can, I'll follow you over, dear.'

'Will you, really?'

'*Of course.*'

'You are good,' she said, and gave him back the cup. 'Thank you.'

And he thought of her journey, miles and miles on slow trains, into the wilderness, as his wife had so often described it to him. He held her hand, whispered into her ear, then got up, extended a smile. 'So sorry about it,' he said. 'I'll help you pack.'

But at this moment Lucy was beyond hearing, and did not even hear her husband leave the room.

'Poor Father,' she said.

And said it again as she sat alone in the compartment, 'Poor Father.' There was a distant sound of hissing steam, and a little later, the sound of hurrying footsteps down the platform. She got up and stood at the window, then quickly closed the door. She thought of the journey, hoped nobody would get in, and took a seat in the corner. How good David was, how helpful, a tower of strength, what on earth would she have done without him? The thoughts seemed to induce a kind of warmth into the compartment. People were now passing by, she heard the opening and closing of doors, and knew she would soon be on her way. She hoped the train for Craven Arms wouldn't be late, and perhaps it might be a little warmer than this one. And then the door swung open, and another passenger joined her. A middle-aged man, well dressed, who sat opposite her, and immediately buried himself in his morning paper. What a relief, thought Lucy, hardly in the mood for talking. She stared at the paper, tried to decipher some black headlines, and then the paper came down, was quickly folded, and the passenger spoke.

'Rough morning.'

'Yes.'

'Going far?'

'Craven Arms,' replied Lucy.

'Ought to do something about the heating, don't you think?' And she wasn't thinking.

'Just look at those windows,' he said, a finger pointing, and angrily. The conversation ceased abruptly when he got out at the next station.

Glad he's gone. Hope nobody else gets in here, don't want to talk to anybody. Poor Cadi. Wonder what she looks like now, such a time.

And the litany of omissions. Should have written, kept in touch. Poor dear.

Wonder what really happened, thinking of the telegram. Sort of curt, seemed to me, and the name, block-lettered, seemed close to her eyes. Evans. Why not *Cadi?*

Yes, she should have kept in touch. She thought of David again, the little miracle, the splendid lifebelt. I was happy, that's what it was, happy. Might still have been living at *that* place, and the very thought only lengthened the journey.

Strange seeing her after all these years, very strange. I'm sixty now. And she... yes, I got my chance, I took it.

She hoped David could arrange something, and follow her on.

Extraordinary feeling came over me when I read it. Felt isolated. She pushed her hands up her sleeve, resettled herself, then lay back, and closed her eyes. The rhythm of the train seemed to synchronise with her thoughts, as she travelled backwards, and the train forward.

And she thought of the quiet, reserved life she had lived over the Post Office in Averton, and of her dutiful, hard-working

61

husband. David himself had few interests, and lived for his work, and it was this that gave him his sole sense of being important. They rarely went out. On his day off they went to the local cinema to see 'what's on', at the Odeon. Occasionally a friend of his would drop in, and they shared a quiet, homely supper, indulging in bright chatter of little consequence. There were occasions when David would talk nothing but 'shop', so giving the impression that Averton covered the entire world. Sometimes, as they sat together in the evening listening to the radio, he would look at her and become deeply aware that he had been the life-saving part of the big adventure, the memorable meeting in a small Prestatyn café. Lucy's lucky day. A miracle day, and a startling confrontation over cups of tea, followed by the initial wave of shyness in both parties. And how honest she had been, telling him her age at that first encounter. What a big woman she was, dwarfing him. Sometimes he saw her only through clouds of smoke, for the pipe rarely left his lips. What friends they had were his, she had none. Tea and cakes having loosened their tongues, she informed him that her father had once been a farrier, but now was 'farming', somewhere in Wales, and he in turn told her of his mother, with whom he had lived, until her passing. And Lucy was left in no doubt concerning his devotion to her. How faithful a son David had been. How lucky she was to have met him by a sheer accident. After which there had followed the questions that had been shrewd, and calculating. And David had readily obliged.

Lucy was so absorbed in these reflections that she hardly noticed the woman passenger, who had got on at a previous station. And she was remembering it all, every little detail of it. What a good job he had with the Post Office.

A wonderful day, she told herself. She had been happy ever since. Hunched over a small table, with its soiled cloth, its filled ashtray, and its colourful plate of cakes, and enjoying their cup of tea, he had informed her that 'you are the one', and he noticed how her face had brightened. In no time at all they were wandering about in each other's lives, and he thought of what a good housekeeper she would make, whilst she threw out a metaphorical hand to grasp the lifebelt he had offered her.

And in a matter of weeks, I'd deserted Father, and married him.

After which great event they were as happy and snug as two doves in a nest, and so wrapped up in each other that she had long forgotten a distant horizon, and the very mileage between Averton Post Office and a holding named Pen y Parc. That place in Wales, and Father there, a question mark at a faraway place. From that day she had known her real anchorage, and never lost the sight or feel of it.

Getting away. I got away.

The train had stopped, the woman passenger departed, and she hardly realized it, as the train jogged on its way to Craven Arms.

Railway seat had become rack as she wandered in her thoughts, back to Averton, forward to Wales. The years? She daren't count them. Turned forty when I met him, and do I say thank God for David? I certainly do.

The very thought seemed to increase the speed of the train. Poor Father. Why did he do it?

And thought of a morning at Ty Coch when the mist lay heavy over the house, and she heard the usual explosion with a great clearness, as yet another horse was shod, and free.

Poor man. He knew more about horses than he ever did about women. Poor Mother. How she spoiled him, that wisp of a woman moving soundlessly about the house, doing her duty. I sometimes think that her happiest moments came to her at a day's end, when at last she could sit herself down in a chair, and stay there.

But there had been another explosion later, after Mother had died. She was lost in the occasion. An explosion that had carried upstairs to her, the message, the ultimatum. He was through with it, the lot, the whole bloody lot of it.

I didn't understand, and I don't now. It was mad, stupid. What *happened?* God! It's as close as close, I can hear him saying it, straight to my face. I was standing at the window at the time, looking down into the lane. So *unthinking.*

He was going away, selling up. Why, going *where?* And what was I to do? Faithful servant. Go with him of course. Hadn't she always been with him, hadn't she always been nearest to him since Mother had died?

I couldn't believe it. He had seen an advert about a vacant holding in the local paper, and on the spur of the moment, bought it. I can see him now, standing close to me.

'A holding,' I said, 'where?'

He told me, and I said. 'You're mad, Father, plain crazy.' Never forget the look he gave me, seemed *surprised*, as if plain common sense was offensive to him. I clutched his arm, began shaking him, 'You can't.' I'll never forget his answer. He almost spoke like a lawyer. He could, and he

64

would. He had had enough of horses, enough of Ty Coch. Mother was gone now, things were different, and he was suddenly sick of the ground on which he stood.

'And you expect me to go with you?' Yes, I can hear myself saying it. He flung it at me. '*Yes*.' And I had to go, what else could I have done?

The days that were gone now rose in clouds in the railway carriage, and through them, all she appeared to see was the pale light from the bulb over her head. And as the train crossed the points, it shook, and the swinging light made lightning patterns on the dirt of the window. The clouds shut her in, the *days* lined the compartment like ghosts. A failure. And where did his silly idea ever get him? 'It all seems like a dream to me,' Lucy said aloud in the carriage, now beginning to warm up. She stood up, a little unsteadily, and went to the window, stared out at the flashing-by telegraph poles, and wished only that they would carry the days with them. Only the hounds remained, and she could not leash them.

And then, suddenly we were there, and I saw it, and my heart sank, and I said to him, 'Is this it?' and he said yes. I went as cold as a stone.

'It's a wilderness, you'll regret this, Father, you know nothing about this kind of life; you're a stranger here, and you've made me one, too.' That was all he wanted, and he stood his stubborn ground.

I thought of the work he did, was best at what he *knew,* all thrown away on a silly whim. I couldn't believe I was actually *there*. He'd asked me to understand him, and I couldn't.

'How d'you suppose I feel, stuck out here, in this place, half a mile up a mountain, *a mountain?*'

How pathetic it all was. And the words again, listening to them. 'We've always been together, Lucy,' he said. 'We must stand by each other, *work*. I'll work.'

'I'm sure you will.'

'It's what I *want*,' he shouted in my face. '*Is that* all? H'm!'

Lucy sat heavily in the seat, longed for the train to arrive, longed to fly from the welter of thoughts that crowded about her. 'And now,' she said, and the thought an iron jolt, 'now, he's gone.'

The load of confidence in that day. No. Nothing would go wrong. *He* knew. Throwing up a home, a living, everything. *Why?*

The way he looked at me, almost begging me to believe him, to accept. And the train dragged on.

Three miserable looking fields, and a broken-down house. And what did he say about *that?* 'It's only the beginning,' he said, and I wanted to laugh my head off when I heard him say it. So earnest, so determined, even his face lit up, he even looked younger than he was, in his *sixties* then.

'It's done,' he said. 'We're here, and I'm going through with it.'

Sounded more like an end to me, than any beginning.

All done in secret, and never a word spoken.

Never asked me what I thought, how I felt. 'You'll rue the day,' I said. How pathetic he looked then, and from that moment I knew he was going to lean heavily on me. My heart sank. I asked myself for how long, and will it be a

66

success, and what will I do? We can't be together forever; I have my life, and I *wanted* my life. I told him straight. Pleaded with him to change his mind, go back, and what did he say to that? 'You mean much to me,' was all he said. And I wondered about that, so much that I didn't even answer him, turned my back on him. I remember being stood at the window, watching it grow dark, and even if it had been bright light, I wouldn't have seen anything *then*.

She writhed in the days that spelt themselves out with unerring regularity.

So it began, so it has ended, a wasted life. The train's whistle made her jump.

There were worse things to come, and he never even saw them coming. It was like I wasn't really *there*, *looking* at him, and forever asking myself where it was going to end. Sometimes I've gone up to my room, and sat there, even looking into the mirror, asking myself who I was. And the things that had to be done. That strange walk through a strange land, right into the village shop to buy the things that were necessary, and that woman. I can see her now, looking at me with questioning eyes, àlmost as if I hadn't the right to be there. Ah, she thought, and the sigh came with it. She's gone, heaven knows who has the place now. And the *walking*, the sheer walking.

The train might never stop, it might go to the end of the world. Was it going round in circles?

Those first days, trying to get some warmth into the house, forever cleaning, and that kitchen garden... God... *that*, the beginning. Father tramping through three little fields, perhaps asking himself what they would bring forth.

67

I thought about it, too. Grass, hay, corn? I used to watch him as he went his way, and the message rising out of the morning. What would that be? I wondered about that also. Before I quite realized it I was pulling on the leash. Those meal times; I'll never forget them. The things he'd say, dropping like omens, stones in a pool. Over and over again, it was what *he* wanted, what he intended to do, get. *I* just listened. I once actually smiled at him, and I'm sure now that he hated it. The rooms were half empty, the furniture, *our* home, turned up in dribs and drabs. Later, some poultry arrived, right out of the blue, a silly dream beginning to work. I cleaned, I cooked, did all that was expected of me, because he was my father, a poor, silly man that had suddenly gone off his head.

She thought of Craven Arms, and cried in her mind: *When?* And back to the window, and those poles still flying past. Only the journey seemed longer, and where *was* Craven Arms? Would the train ever get there? I'll never forget the first Sunday there. 'It's Sunday,' I said. He *knew* that. Would he go to chapel? No. Would I? It shocked me then. I said no, because I could never have said yes, walking into a company of strangers, against my will, planted out in this place, and I repeated that I wouldn't. I asked him if he'd met anybody. 'Not yet,' he said, and I snapped back at him, saying, 'You'll have to.' 'I will,' he said. How glad I used to be when a day ended. Some evenings it was just like a little oasis, that was when he sat in his chair, and puffed contentedly at his pipe, and read his daily paper. And he did read. I used to get his paper for him in the village. One morning I got the surprise of my life when the woman in the shop said, 'Good

68

morning,' such a surprise, and it made me feel better in a flash, just those two little words. Another morning I went out and found two barrows on the step; we were settling in, settling *down*. Things were beginning to shape themselves, and I was involved in them, and all the time I didn't want to be involved in anything. I just wanted to go away, clear right out of the place. I didn't, for bits of his dream were now beginning to stick to me, and the days grew and the days passed us by. And at last he did meet *somebody*. *A* man had actually come to plough for him. After that he was digging, and scraping, and I can see him coming in of an evening, with hardly a word out of him. I thought to myself, One evening he'll come back and tell me what he's been doing, anything, perhaps that something was beginning to *grow*. I'd sit opposite him after supper. And what did we talk about? The damned weather, and too often. I was sick of the weather, and the house, and the fields, and the mountain. Sometimes I didn't want to speak to a living soul.

One afternoon I walked into the back kitchen to start making a meal, and I found him standing at the sink, his head bent, staring out of the little window. His hands gripping the board as he stood there, stone still. And then what I saw, I couldn't believe. He was crying, and it scared me. I went away and left him standing there. Later, things were back to normal, and I never asked any questions, a surprising incident. I even began to feel sorry for him, the way he went on, secretly hoping, I suppose, though I was determined not to give way. I was afraid of losing my own nerve, for I knew, suddenly, that I would never give way, and as true as God's in heaven, that one day I would walk out on him, and leave him for good. I had my life to live, too.

David came back, filled the whole carriage, the good man, the sensible man. And she thought of the strange *way* they had first met.

'It was fate. I know it was.'

She cried this aloud in the stuffy carriage, and at last heard the shrill whistle, but her husband was still there, close beside her. Living the essence of an occasion, the new day, that wonderful hour. Suppose it had never happened, she asked herself, as it set alive the thoughts of that particular day, and of what, some days later, she had left behind. How would things have gone. What would her father have done? Remained in the groove that he'd made for himself through an act of stupidity.

A sudden explosion of energy, of sheer noise, struck and roused her. 'Are you getting out here, madam?'

Madam, she thought, and looked up, confused, staring at the porter in the doorway, who said in a quiet voice, 'Craven Arms, madam.'

'*Oh!* Is it? Thank you,' and she reached up, fingers clutching her case, whilst the porter remained standing there, and asking in the same quiet voice, 'Where are you for, madam?'

And she told him as she stepped down to the platform, staring up and down.

And the voice again. 'Platform two, madam.'

'Yes, thank you,' Lucy said, made to smile, then didn't, and hurried off to platform two. And the hounds followed.

Another train, another compartment, and two women in it. She got in, sat down, did not look at them, hearing only the blast of steam from the engine. She lay back, closed her eyes, heard this train move. At last. Off again. What a journey.

One of the women opposite had a bout of coughing, and Lucy opened her eyes, looked at them both, closed them again, forgot them, and she hoped that neither of them would speak to her.

I was so used to being where I was wanted, always attendant. And then it happened, unexpected, right out of the blue. I'll never forget that day, always remember it, set me free. Almost funny how it happened. I had to go into the village one afternoon, just to order and carry back the things that were necessary, and I used to do this about once a month. That woman in Central Stores had all of a sudden become different, and for the first time I didn't feel a stranger. And that first smile she ever gave me, I knew I was a person. I paid for my things, picked up the bag, and had almost reached the door when she called me back. I wondered why. Also, and for the first time, she actually spoke my name.

'Miss Evans,' she said, and it was like warmth, hearing it.
'Yes?'

'There happens to be a spare ticket for a charabanc trip to Prestatyn. Would you like to have it?'

I couldn't believe my ears; it confused me for a moment. Would I like to have it? Prestatyn. I'd heard of the place, by the sea. A trip for the day. Wonderful. When she looked at me, I just smiled back, and she knew the answer. So did I hear of the run to the sea. Women only. I suddenly hedged, for I didn't know a soul in the place, except one or two people passing me by in the lane. How would I get on? What would they think of me, say? Yes, and what would they think of Father, the stranger just come in?

'Yes, I'll take the ticket. I'll go. What time; what day?'

71

'Friday,' she replied, 'meet outside the Half Moon, twelve noon.'

Half Moon? Never heard of it. And then I was asking her all kinds of questions. She told me, and I paid for my ticket, and hurried back home. It was like sailing on air. But walking back I suddenly had doubts. What would Father say? I could laugh about it now, since when I got back I just told him, simply and directly that I was going off for the day. I thought he'd explode, but he didn't – perhaps it sounded like a fairy tale to him at the time. But the backlash came later, for I couldn't conceal my own excitement about getting away on my own. He sulked the rest of the day; never said a word. But on his way to bed, he paused half way up the stairs, then came slowly down, stood over me, and I've never seen such an expression as he wore. I spoke before he did.

'I've never been there in my life, never even *seen* the sea,' I said.

'And you want to go?'

The way he said it, deep in his throat, struggling with the words as though he hated them, and went on glaring at me, I couldn't look at him any longer. I knew he was only thinking of himself. 'You really intend to go?'

I shouted it at him, 'Yes,' I said, 'Yes.'

And the worst was over. I could hardly settle down that night. The very thought of being out of his sight, on my own, talking to other people. Nothing like this had ever happened before, and in the end I fell happily asleep. When I woke, my thoughts were leaden. I dreaded going downstairs, having to sit opposite him for breakfast, yes, and the moment I did I saw the resentment there. It didn't surprise me. We'd lived such a quiet, ordinary life, all this was a new adventure to me, and for the first time I began to feel like a real person. He ate in silence, and I didn't care, and that night I took a pleasurable feeling with me to my bed. Just the thought of getting *away* for a few hours. Wonderful.

And she saw the morning, and the bus, and the country rolling by, and listened to the bright chatter of the passengers.

Remember I sat beside a much older woman, tiny she was, introduced herself to me as a Mrs Humphreys. She talked of nothing but this trip, and how they did it once a year. Yes, it was always arranged by Central Stores. The one day in the year when the women got away from the men. The way she chatted on. She told me that a Mr Ellis sometimes accompanied them, but wasn't coming this year. I sat there, listening with one ear only, for the other was filled with the voices of the other people, some of whom never stopped talking.

Lucy suddenly stirred in her seat, looked up, but hardly seemed to see the two passengers sat opposite her. And she thought of old Mrs Humphreys with a quiet affection, and wondered what had happened to her.

'Perhaps after the meal we could have a walk round the town,' she'd said. Lord! I can hear her saying it this very moment, I nodded, and we exchanged smiles. It was becoming a dream trip.

'Never been there in my life,' I told her.

'You haven't, dear?' she said, as though the news had shocked her. 'I always enjoy coming, and the mister's always decent about it, being only once a year.'

Prestatyn. What a cheery place. And the people, and the noise, the shouting and laughing going on. And the smell of the sea. Always remember that. The lunch was lovely, and we did go for a walk along the beach. Everything was exciting, and Pen y Parc had gone right out of my head. The crowds, never seen such for a long time. Yes, and that's how I lost sight of Mrs Humphreys, poor old dear. So once again I seemed to be walking about amongst strangers, and I'd quite forgotten half the faces on the bus. I wanted to sit down somewhere, but all the seats seemed occupied. I went back into the town, and walked up and down the streets, always hoping to bump into my friend. At last I stopped at a small café, and looking through the window I could see it was crowded, too. But I went in, and I did manage to find a table. And there was a man already seated at it. It was David.

'David,' she said aloud, to the instant surprise of the passengers, and further surprised them when they saw her put the flat of her hands to her face, and press them there.

Talking to herself, thought one, and the other said, 'Are you going far?'

'Craven Arms,' replied Lucy, and her hands fell flat to her lap. She felt shy, ashamed. 'Must have nodded off,' she said, and smiled at them, and they smiled back.

'Awful slow train.'

'They all are these days.'

'Is it very far?' asked Lucy.

'Three more stations,' said the taller woman. 'Thank you.'

'Welcome.'

They got out at the next station, and she was alone again.

I can see him now, getting up and standing back whilst I sat down. I was glad of the tea when it came. And as I stirred

74

it, I noticed him looking hard at me, but I did not look up at once, but began drinking my tea. When I did he was still looking, and then he actually smiled. I knew he was older, and he looked it, but there was something attractive about the man. He was without a hat, and his grey hair brushed neatly back. He wore pince-nez. Yes, I can even see those gloves of his lying at the corner of the table. He began to talk then, about the weather, then asked me how far I'd come, and I told him. He said he came from a place called Averton, told me his name, said Averton was in Cheshire, and laughed then, saying, 'Where everything's flat.' The things he began to do, helping me to more tea, holding out the cakes, so attentive, smiling again. I wasn't used to it, and I couldn't conceal my pleasure. I think he noticed it right away. Suddenly he was leaning across the table, being more intimate, started talking about his mother, and his whole expression changed. Yes, he'd lost her. We just talked on, and I quite forgot the time. And the enquiries. Did I often come to Prestatyn, and I said it was the first time I'd even seen the sea. He looked earnestly at me, and I was nervous then, as he said quite casually, 'I like you.'

I felt silly for a moment or two, too surprised I was, then I said, 'Do you, really?'

I was so taken up by the way he was looking at me that I never noticed how near his hand was to mine. He stopped talking, and then I turned my head away. I couldn't sit there, so close, with him silent. 'I told you my name,' he said suddenly, and then I remembered he had. I trembled a bit, and then said, 'I'm Lucy Evans.'

How prompt he was, and that smile again. 'I'm pleased to meet you, Miss Evans.'

It did something to me, it really did, and I couldn't remember a time when somebody had said that to me. And he continued talking, telling me about himself. How lonely he'd been since his mother died, and how he'd longed to meet somebody like myself. His change of expression told me that he'd even surprised himself.

I stiffened where I sat, couldn't speak a word, just listened as he went on and on. And again and again about how lonely he'd been. It was another world. For a split second my mind went back to Father, the house, and my heart sank. Then I looked at him, and said quite boldly, 'I like you, too, Mr Stevens.'

'David,' he said, and his hand was covering mine. I blushed, felt awkward, and it seemed to produce such a smile, and he said, 'Do call me David.'

I did, and he called me Lucy, I never felt so happy before. 'We must meet again,' he said.

I didn't answer because I was too astonished, and something was happening inside me. I thought of his age, of my own, and then I thought of Father again, and that wilderness. I felt angry and sad, and happy, all at the same time. Then there were more questions, and more answers.

'I've come on a bus trip for the day, David,' I said. 'I'm leaving at five o'clock.'

His face fell. '*What* a pity. I'm here for three days myself. I used to go to Rhyl once a year, but I like this place much better. Yes, and then back to the job.'

I didn't feel shy any more, asked him about his work, and he told me more about himself. He was the Sub-Postmaster, and he had a nice big flat over it. He had sold his house when his mother passed away. And back again to how he felt so lonely since being on his own. It was when he smiled again that I asked myself if perhaps the whole thing wasn't just a little game to him. He'd broken free for three days, I for a few hours. But I *was* touched by the things he said, way he looked at me, seemed open and honest enough to me, and I liked his manners. Perhaps I shouldn't believe any of it, too sudden, too surprising, even upsetting in a way. When I looked up at the clock I got a real shock, and was restless at once, and he noticed it. Leaning close again. Would I like another cup of tea, a cake? By this time I didn't want to go at all, looking at him, thinking about it, liking him.

And I thought of David all the way home, and that night I carried the pleasurable experience up to my room, and it was like freshness there; it was new, and the things I forgot. Ty Coch, my Mother, the forge, my own father. Just like walking from a dark room to one that was full of light. Something was actually *happening* to me. Poor Father sitting at the table, and looking everywhere but directly at me, and it didn't matter, I was still full of my day out, and then I talked and talked about it, couldn't stop. To this day I don't believe he was even listening. And then he wasn't there. It was David Stevens sitting there. 'You'd have loved it,' I said, and when I looked again it was Father, and David had vanished.

He ate his supper in silence, and I wondered if I'd ever finish my own. He got up quickly, walked away, did not say goodnight, and the moment he'd gone, I'd gone, too. I was back in that café, listening to a stranger talking to me. And I wasn't sitting on a chair, but on air.

77

'Perhaps I'll send you a card,' David said. How well I remember that. He looked so hopeful when he smiled, and I thought to myself, Perhaps there is going to be a tomorrow for me, too. How I clung to that. In the end I gave him my address, and he gave me his in Averton. First time I'd heard of the place. Perhaps it was somewhere on the Border. And that was new as well, and I felt a real country bumpkin. 'Pity you have to go back,' he said, and I said yes, and he gave a little sigh. 'Ah well, there'll be another time,' and this remark made me think of the things he *hadn't* said. A new feeling came over me, and then I wanted to be quite ruthless, accept the challenge. 'I'll write, Miss Evans,' he said, paused, then stuttered out, *'Lucy.'*

'I'll write, too.'

And he did, and so did I.

Her body was inert in the seat, but her thoughts were miles away.

He did write. Lord! Most beautiful surprise I ever had. Actually writing to *me*. So I wrote back at once. And he wrote again.

She thought of early-morning walks into twisting little lanes, watching for the postman. For he daren't come near the door. I was so certain in my mind about what he might be thinking, his odd way of looking at me when I collected a letter. Different the moment he'd gone. Opening that letter, the words dancing in front of me, and the things he was saying. *Real.*

'I've been thinking quite a lot, Miss Evans,' he wrote, 'since we last met, may I call you Lucy?' And there was lots more, and I read on. I knew then that it was all or nothing, and I summoned up my courage, for my head was now full of a postmaster in Averton. The thoughts leapt in and out of my head. What would his next letter say? That he wanted to marry me? How I wondered on that. Was it true? Would it happen? So there were more letters, more early-morning walks to meet that postman who was now so curious, and I didn't care; I had the big secret, and Father hadn't a clue, for he never left his bed until I'd given him his morning cup of tea. Then the moment he went out I'd fling David's letter into the flames. I had to make up my mind, knew it was now or never, but I didn't push, and was careful to hide my inner excitement. It was an adventure, and I had to be careful; I thought a lot about that. I realized that we scarcely knew each other, and perhaps there were still things he hadn't told me. Things had happened to people before, I knew that, so I didn't immediately reply to the next letter. And that postman had become real suspicious now; it made me feel awful.

I began to think deeply about it then, for every word in his letters was now clear to me. Would I come and meet him at Averton? Seemed such a distance away. And all this time Father was ignorant of what was going on, what was pressing on my mind, the plan I was dreaming up. There were some awful moments, too, when I began to dread what I was thinking of. I told myself, 'careful', the whole thing might fall to pieces. And there was something about Father, I felt he was quietly pulling at me. I could almost imagine him suddenly asking me, 'What's going on?' Then I wondered whether I'd have the nerve to tell him straight out, 'I'm going away to get married; I'm leaving you.'

How would he look; what would he say? Accuse me of deserting him, being cruel, yes, I *was* his daughter, and since Mother'd gone, always close. And how much he depended on me. I could see the whole thing happening now. Which it did, of course.

We weren't at Ty Coch now. All was different. I hadn't asked to come. He had forced the situation on me, and I still thought he was mad. *He* had opened my eyes at last. Different for him. He was a *man*. Over and over and over it went; my mind rocked with it all. And I was still trying to make up my mind, get it off my chest for good. It was then that I was determined to reply to his letter, and I thought about it the whole day and all that night, looking at it from every single angle I could. It was my last chance to have a new life, *my* life. And the next morning was *very* different.

He watched me all through breakfast, I him. All he said was 'Good morning,' I the same. Yet the expression on his face unnerved me. Was he wondering what I was thinking? That look. I can see it now, peering at me over the rim of his cup, and not drinking his tea. Not a word spoken, just watching, and perhaps, waiting, and the expression spoke to me. 'What is it, what are you thinking of, *now* this moment; what's happening, there's something going on in that head of yours.' I avoided his eyes, glanced at everything except him, anything to dodge that long, steady look of his, and me thinking of the word that might pop out, getting an inkling, a sudden catching out. My God! Was I relieved when he said very quietly, 'We'd best get on,' and got up and walked out of the house. So we just got on, the big garden again. After a while he left me without a word, and I followed his figure across the field, and then he stopped, stood leaning on the gate. What was *he* thinking? In this new place, this strange place, into which I'd been whirled at a moment's notice. I ruminated about it as I went on digging.

Write it tonight, slip it in the box early in the morning, before that postman comes near, get it done, yes, yes, and *yes*, *I will*, I must. I'd made up my mind at last. He had nothing to say when he came in to his midday meal, just that he thought I'd done well with the garden. Nothing more. I said a good garden was everything, one needn't starve, or something to that effect. The place was beginning to look shipshape as they say, everything had now turned up from Ty Coch, and we spent days putting things in their place. I was glad, too, that he hadn't got rid of the grandfather clock; I thought he might, and it looked so nice in the corner. I think it was valuable, but the only attention he ever paid it was to wind it regularly. Suddenly he started talking about the things he was going to do, little plans he had in mind. That very afternoon a man called with the daily paper that I'd quite forgotten to collect from the village, and they went off down the path together, then the man turned and looked at me, then back again to Father, and I really hated his voice when he cried out, laughing at the same time, 'You'll get a fine crop of rabbits come summer,' and Father laughed, too. I'm sure they both thought it was funny.

I counted the seconds, the minutes, the hours, I thought of my room, being in it, writing that letter, getting a firm grip on my freedom, thinking of my tomorrow. And still Father gave no hint at all of what he knew, might know, felt. No sign. Besides he didn't seem suspicious, either. He was always a punctual man, off to bed at the same time every night, and I always listened for the loud creak on the fifth stair. Off he went with a gruff, 'Goodnight' leaving me sat by the fire. I could hear him moving about upstairs, but I sat tight until he'd settled down. Always took the paper to bed with him, only half read it during the day. Sometimes I've seen his lamp on till after midnight. The lamp over my head suddenly went out, and I never bothered to light it again, the fire was bright enough. Then I heard the thud of his boots on the floor, and knew he was actually in bed. I waited a while longer, damped down the fire, locked the door, and went up to my room. There I wrote a long letter to David, and just writing it cheered me up no end; every word I wrote, I meant. I slept with it under my pillow, and I didn't go to sleep for a long time, just *lay* there, thinking and thinking. I examined the reasons for my decision, and I didn't have to defend myself any longer, I just knew I was right. It would teach Father a lesson, force him to stand up straight, do something for himself, for in all the years we were together things were expected of me, and if I wasn't determined, might go on forever. My freedom might start him thinking of what he had done, his own life, and what to do with it, without me, without a woman. It would do him good, me even better.

I was up at my usual time, heard him snoring as I passed his door, crept downstairs, and was off to the pillar box in the wink of an eye. It was quite dark, but I knew where I was going, and I dropped the letter into the box. But the moment I did it, I was loaded with doubt, all over again. And for the first time I thought of the distance to Averton. Could I make it in a day?

A long way, would it happen? And it did, and it was a very long letter that I posted to him three days later, and I explained all the difficulties. Just putting it into the box cheered me up. When his next letter arrived, and I read it, well away from the house, I just couldn't believe it. He explained everything, what to do, where to be, his plan. He had a little car, and in one week's time he would meet me in a lane well away from the house, and when it was quite dark. It sounded so easy, so final to me. All I had to do was meet him, get into the car, and we'd be away. 'Away,' I kept saying to myself. Later the very simplicity of the thing made me nervous again, but not for long, for my excitement grew, and at the same time I was feeling furious with myself, but without understanding why.

That very night I wrote Father a letter, told him everything, and I was so buoyed up, that I even gave him some advice. To get married, and he'd have all the help he wanted. It was done. I was free. Ah! I think I'll always remember that morning when a woman in a village shop asked me if I'd like to go on a day trip to Prestatyn. Father *never* understood what it was like being a woman. One week later I slipped away from the house, left him. And it all happened as David said it would, and my spirit shot up at once. I'll always remember sitting in this kitchen, and outside a big cardboard box behind the bushes containing my things. Sat a whole hour, waiting. Soon as his lamp went out, I put on hat and coat, and left the house; the letter I'd written I stood against the sugar basin on the table. I went down that path as though a whole fleet of devils was after me. Black dark, but I knew where to go. Suddenly there it was. A light shining in the distance, and I knew it could only

83

be the headlights of a car. I started to run, and only one single dread inside me, that it might be the wrong car. It wasn't, and I came to it, and there he was, in his top coat and hat, pince-nez and all. Smiled his way out of the car, took my hands, squeezed them, then for the first time, kissed me. My head swam. I never experienced such a moment before. Excited and pleased with myself having the courage to do it, and I was as close as ever I would get to this man, David. I even imagined that behind a long hedge, people were hiding, watching and listening. We spoke in whispers, then he gave an odd laugh, and looked at his watch.

'Now, dear,' he said.

The feeling I got from two words. The car moved off into the darkness, and you could hardly see a thing in front of you, what with a heavy mist coming down. I couldn't quite believe it, I was close to him at the wheel, and we both talked and talked. And I wasn't going directly to his home, he'd fixed me up in an hotel for the night. He would come there the next evening, and we'd talk again. 'Lots of talk,' he said. Once he stopped the car and held both my hands, gave me a strange feeling. So for the very first time I found myself in an hotel, and a maid took me to my room, and told me what time she'd bring up breakfast. It was like a fairy tale. And I never slept on such a comfortable bed, the room lovely and warm. The next morning there she was with the tray. After breakfast I went out and had a look at Averton. Immediately I felt a stranger again, but I enjoyed the shops, and all the people hurrying along this way and that, so lively. That evening I sat on a couch and waited for David. There were two other people sitting there, and we smiled at each other, but didn't speak, for I felt far too shy to open my mouth. As for the clock over my head, I never took my eyes off it. This was it, one way or the other. Then promptly at half past six he walked into the foyer. Was I glad to see him? It was still like a dream, the whole business. That didn't last very long, for he took me into another room, and asked me what I'd like to have. I said lemonade. He came back with this, and a whisky for himself. There was just one awful moment between us, as if we were both uncertain, but when we sat down the practical side of the man came out at once. Then he covered my hand with his own, looked steadily at me, and then said, 'Are you quite sure in your own mind?' Surprised me in a way, but I told him I was, and felt happy after that. And he went on talking. I listened. We'd go off to Chester, and get married in a Registry Office, and after that we'd go somewhere for a whole week, and then he'd take me home. 'Home,' I thought. 'Home,' I said. It had *happened*. Just at that moment a man came up to us, older than David, tall, a very well dressed gentleman, saluted David, gave me an instant enquiring glance, and said, 'So here we are, David.'

How real it was, and I remember every incident, every word of that day. 'Lucy, this is my friend, George Penfold, he works at the Post Office, too. He knows all about it, and he's going to be witness at our wedding.'

For a moment I was too bewildered to say anything, and then he left me to go and get a drink for Mr Penfold. The moment he'd gone, the man started talking to me. He said something in such a casual way that at first it quite upset me, talked about David's mother, how upset he'd been.

'I've been advising him for some time now, Miss Evans, to look around for a good housekeeper.'

I couldn't look at the man, and I never forgot what he said, nor the moment he said it. Then David came back with the drink. Such a relief, and I felt better after that, but I still felt sort of angry inside me at what Mr Penfold had said, and so *casually*. David kept looking at me, so affectionately, and Mr Penfold held up his glass, wished us both health and good luck. Then he went off, and David saw him to the door. I can't explain how glad I was that he'd gone.

'Who is Mr Penfold?' I asked.

'But didn't I tell you. He's Post Office like me, though a distance away, known him for years, a good chap.'

'Is he married?'

'Of course, and a family, Lucy. Nice people. We'll all meet one day.'

Being alone together was a relief, though I still kept thinking of what the man had said to me. I think David noticed something, too, the way he looked at me, and asked if everything was all right, was I worried about something, and the warmth again. 'Dear,' he said, and I thought to myself, 'You're being plain silly, he does mean what he says, he does want to marry me.'

'I'm not worried about a thing,' I said.

He passed a hand over his forehead, and exclaimed abruptly, 'For a moment I thought you'd changed your mind. Did you like my friend?'

'Seems a nice enough man,' was all I could say in reply.

'*Do* have a glass of wine,' he said, 'just to celebrate the occasion,' and when I smiled my answer he went off and came back with a bottle of wine.

'Like it?'

'Very nice,' I said, though I was really asking myself if it was.

86

Suddenly he was serious again, and leaning very close.

'You're not regretting anything, Lucy?' he asked, his mouth partly open, and I saw his teeth, and knew at once that they weren't his own.

I hesitated for a second, suddenly thinking of Father. And I wondered why he had never mentioned him. 'I regret nothing,' I said.

'The nicest thing,' he said, 'was meeting you, Lucy.'

I remember my eyes moistening, I was so touched by what he said. I'm sure I blushed. He pushed his handkerchief at me.

'Come along, dear,' he said, and it made him seem husband and father and brother all at the same time. 'Nothing to cry about.'

I shook my head, was shy again in an instant, looking away from him. I could feel him very close then, and he said, 'We're going to be happy, Lucy.'

'Yes,' and he held my hands tight again. 'Not everyone would have done what you've done for me,' he said.

The way he said it to me, and somehow I sensed that he really meant it, and I thought hard about that, too.

And it happened. Yes, we got off, and we did get married, Chester it was, as he said, and after that we went to an hotel for a meal. Later we went to the Lakes. How I remember that. It rained the whole time we were there, but I didn't mind it in the least. Strange in a way. My! The way things happen. Just a little accident, really, but it helped me to find a way out, be myself at last.

4

How long have I been sitting here?

And Cadi didn't know, and she didn't want to get up, but sat on at the table, staring at the papers strewn across it, and some she had picked up without even a glance at them, then let them fall from her hand. The way she sat, the position of her hands, and the very expression she wore, bespoke a kind of listlessness, a sudden retreat from former resolution, an unwillingness to examine the contents of this canister. Day after day, a letter, a receipt, money, was tossed into it, and then forgotten. And here it was, all back again, and the litter of days with it. Once she stiffened herself, sat up, thought she would burn the lot, then suddenly closed her eyes. The moment told her that she was strangely alone. Lucy was forgotten, had passed beyond a horizon of her mind.

I never once asked him why he came here, and I'm glad. I accepted everything that happened to me, and I spoke only when I was spoken to. I've changed, I know I have; so many things have ceased to be of any importance to me.

Her fingers fastened on a piece of paper, and she opened her eyes, looked at it, bent close, read it, a worn piece of paper, a tattered receipt. *Jan 6th. Central Stores. Two buckets, one bag of staples, one spade.* Spade, she thought. 'Spade,' she said, and a man rose up from the paper, and she was far from the house, digging. Bent over a wet ditch, and digging, digging. It was like that, the soil demanding, and if she looked up she would see an afternoon hedge already glistening with frost. But she did not hear a movement behind her, and saw herself jump with fright, heard the voice behind her back.

'Hee hee! Still trying to dig out the devil, Miss Evans?'

And the man, and the voice known. So she swung round, dropping the spade, staring at an intruder, a man come swiftly past her, laughing as he went, legs well apart, and a cap wildly askew upon his head, striding. Where? One known to her, and known to all, and often bent like others to the same compelling soil.

And I said to myself, where next will he stride, what for, what to do? The piece of paper in a hand now become fist, as slowly she squeezed it into the tiniest ball, let it fall to the floor, ignored it.

Poor Twm Pugh. And Father actually wanted me to marry that lunatic, and saying it, she saw him clear, on another day. The shy one, and the grin that often extended from ear to ear. The bringer of unwanted bouquets. So she saw him, on different days, a hand turned fist that clutched tightly to a small bunch of daisies, and once to three daffodils. Saw one of different colours from an October hedge, and remembered also a small bundle that would remain forever twigs.

Fancy me thinking of him now, at this table, he must be around fifty-three... and he came yet closer, this latest helper to Mr Hughes. 'Twm, always helping.'

The man that did anything, anytime, and sometimes, on the very spur of the moment. And there he was, as clear as daylight, standing behind that very table, staring at her. And saw him also stood outside her window, and watched him there, stiffly stood, looking violently from right to left, the eternal posy, bending down, laying it on the step. The shadow of a smile came and vanished as she saw him turn and run down the path, as though for his very life.

And I'll see him again this evening, she thought, when they bring the box. I'll watch him climb stairs behind Mr Hughes.

And she wondered if then, he would grin at her father flat, as he sometimes did at him erect. A man from the day before yesterday, risen up out of a piece of paper. Working for anybody and everybody, in all seasons of a year, asking no questions, and answering none. Cadi raised a finger to her forehead, and slowly tapped it.

He went somewhere long ago, but nobody knows where.

Another receipt in her hand, making her think of walks to a village. *Groceries, more staples, one more bucket.*

And wondered, over fifteen years, how many buckets of stones she had carried from a field.

'Grown in the night, like mushrooms.'

She turned, glanced at Lucy, but she did not disturb her. Silent Lucy. And never even said why she had deserted Father. And I shan't ask her. Doesn't explain a long silence, and I shan't ask her about that, either.

A little book in her hand, with a bright yellow cover. Reading it. *The Missions to Africa.*

Africa. Worlds away. Opening it, reading the pages, the months, years. One shilling a time. She closed the book; she closed her eyes. Miss Jones. And there she was, raincoated, and the same hat, the usual smile. The crusading Miss Jones, tramping the country in all weathers, on behalf of unfortunate ones in distant lands.

I always looked forward to her calling.

And thought of afternoon tea, newly baked scones, home-made bread and butter. Miss Jones bringing with her bright chatter, and the news from behind a mountain.

I shall always remember when she brought that man. Tall, slim, black-haired. I think his eyes were really steel-grey. A surprising afternoon, the sun out, and the lane shining after rain. The yellow-backed book fell from her hand, but she held on to a surprising afternoon. And saw her now, as she opened the door.

'Hello, Cadi.'

'Hello, Miss Jones.'

'How nice it's turned out, hasn't it?'

Waiting on the step, a man by her side, abruptly turning to him. 'You haven't met Mr Davies, I'm sure. Ivor, this is Madog Evans's daughter...'

'Do come in, Miss Jones, Mr...'

'Davies, dear,' Miss Jones said, and preceded her companion into the kitchen.

And the perennial compliments, and Miss Jones smiling, whilst the man stood awkwardly by the dresser.

'How nice you keep everything, Cadi,' the admiring eyes taking in everything. 'Not like those Vaughans at Tree Top, d'you know, Cadi, the times I've been there, and their table never seems to be cleared.'

'Do sit down,' Cadi said, and fussed with a chair for Mr Davies, and he, shyly, sat at the table.

'I always enjoy my tea here,' Miss Jones said, studying Ivor.

The way he stared at me, reflected Cadi, I didn't know where to look, and then Miss Jones popped into the scene again as she served the tea.

'Nice,' Mr Davies said, trying a scone.

'Glanceirw gave me a cheque for the Midland,' announced Miss Jones. 'Very good they are, always gives me a cheque. I heard from Mr Jenkins they may be leaving soon, going to Canada of all places, think of that, Cadi. Toronto. *Miles* away.'

'I hadn't heard a word about it,' said Cadi, and out of the corner of her eye watched Mr Davies drink his tea. How brown he was, how different, thinking of one from Tybaen, and another from Llys.

'I expect you'll be at the Institute Fete next week, Cadi,' said Miss Jones.

'More tea, Miss Jones?'

'Please.'

'Yes,' said Cadi, 'my best customers for the butter.'

'You make such nice butter.'

'What part of Africa are you in, Mr Davies?'

'About a hundred miles outside Nairobi,' he replied, and, smiling, helped himself to another scone. 'Very quiet up here,' he added. Laughing, Miss Jones said there was hardly any need to tell Cadi that.

She looked at the clock, and Mr Davies looked at his watch.

'Time to go, dear,' Miss Jones said, and she bent down for her handbag. Out came the book, the pencil was poised, 'Usual,' she said. Cadi got up and took a shilling from the canister.

'Wish it could be more, Miss Jones.'

'Tut tut.'

Mr Davies rose, collected his hat, and turning to Cadi said how much he had enjoyed his tea.

'Right,' said Miss Jones, pocketed her book. 'I always enjoy your tea.' She looked up at Ivor. 'Ready?'

Cadi followed them to the door, stood there watching them hurry to the gate, at which they both turned, gave a final wave, and were gone.

Cadi sat back in the chair, covered her face. The day was there, the Institute, Miss Jones and Ivor Davies, and the people chattering away, crossing and recrossing the small field. Another surprising day, because he was *there*.

I liked him. I'm sure he liked me, the thought like a pain, and I wished and I wished, and the day died the moment he was gone. And the next day, the usual again, the old groove. She thought of the letter he had sent from Africa, and of one she had written. It had been like something beginning to grow, a new horizon, anchoring, deep down.

And more letters, messages on the wind, wearing time away.

I loved getting them.

Secret readings in her room, and wondering, always wondering.

Shall I talk to Father, tell him?

Her hands came slowly down, the head bent low.

No. I never did, because it never mattered.

She seemed unaware that her head was lying on this table, and that she was actually murmuring into the wood itself.

Another letter and another, and yet another. All the way from Africa, still formal, careful, still 'Dear Miss Evans,' and watching herself run up to the room that was always hers.

Remembering it, holding on to it, and the pain again. The silence was sudden, *awful*.

Remembering, and not wanting to, the eyes staring down, the mouth partly open, but the words could not come, drowned in the instant and consuming rage. Her hand reached out to the little yellow book, and she tore at it, and tore and tore again, and watched it go from her hand, shred by shred.

That last one... that last... care of Miss Jones. And why not direct to me, *me?*

Saw Miss Jones striding up the path, hearing her knock, smiling her in, watching her take a letter from her bag.

She looked so shy as she gave it me. The words are in my ear.

'Came last evening, dear, such a surprise. I was certain I gave Ivor your address...'

'He had it, he had it, his letters came here, to me, *direct.'*

'Well, I don't understand,' Miss Jones said.

And I said nothing, *knew*, I cried in my mind as I looked at her, stood against the dresser.

'He *did* know, Cadi.'

Did. That word. Something finished, and I listened to her chatter, and I was mystified.

'*Read* it, dear.'

'*I shan't.'*

'Why?'

And the screech that upset Miss Jones.

'I said I shan't,' and I said it to her face. I knew. *Felt* it. No afternoon tea, no scones, only a single letter. I couldn't look at her, couldn't move.

The day flashed by, but the moment was clear. I kept crying in my mind, Go, go.

Did *she* know? How?

'Leave me *alone, Miss* Jones,' I said. And she left me alone. A careful beginning, a careful end.

I only read it half way through, and I threw it in the fire. He wasn't coming back, ever. What struck him, struck me. And that was the *man*.

I didn't even know she'd *gone*. And I just stood there, staring at the wall in front of me. I really cried then. I really did.

The hands moved, were now drawing the papers into a small heap, and then she pressed hard on it.

It was with some effort that she now stood up, the papers crushed in her hands, took them to the fire, flung them in, and suddenly shouted, *'Lucy!'*

The papers exploded to flame, and it was the light from these across her face that made Lucy jump with fright. 'Whatever's the *matter*, Cadi?'

Cadi, who wanted to cry in her sister's face, "Everything", bent over her and whispered, 'Nothing.'

'I thought you'd gone out.'

'I did, and I'm back. And I've burnt everything,' replied Cadi.

'Oh dear!'

'I've been sat there half the afternoon. You were fast asleep, dear.'

'Me?'

'Snoring like an elephant.'

'*Cadi!*'

'You were, dear. And look at the time.'

'I told you a lie this morning, Cadi. I didn't sleep well last night.'

'Wish I could have done better. Would you like supper now, or will you wait until after they've gone.'

'Who?'

'Do wake up, dear. Mr Hughes and the man with him.'

'Yes, yes, of course. Let's wait till they've gone, Cadi.'

Cadi, going out, called back. 'I'm sure David will come.'

But Lucy said nothing. 'We're shut in,' she told herself, 'can't move, nowhere to go, nobody *calls*, and her sitting silent at that table half the afternoon. Didn't even bother to wake me up.'

And she longed for a knock.

'It's like a spell, and I feel sort of sick.'

It was then that the gate clicked, and she leapt to her feet, ran to the door, opened it, saw a man coming up the path.

'It's David, at last, God, I'm so relieved,' she cried. 'Cadi! Cadi!'

Cadi came back, stood close to her sister, and then exclaimed, 'Why, it's the doctor, dear. I told you he'd call. Hello, Doctor Morgan, do come in.'

'I shan't stay long,' he said, and stepped inside, glanced at the big woman standing there, turned to Cadi, dropped his voice, said, 'Mrs Stevens?'

Cadi nodded. 'This is my sister, doctor,' and pulled out a chair.

'I'll leave you for a minute,' she said, and Lucy looked across at the doctor.

96

'How do you do, Mrs Stevens, sorry I couldn't come earlier; you've come a long way.'

'I have. What happened, doctor?'

'Rather a bad fall, and at his age. Unfortunately pneumonia set in. We did our best.'

'Thank you.'

'Hadn't been well for some time, Mrs Stevens, a very tired man. I often wondered why he came here. The last two tenants barely scraped a living from the place.'

'My father bought it.'

'Yes... I did know. And now I must go. I expect Cadi's done everything. She was a great help to him, a great help, and I hope in some way it will console you.'

Lucy followed him to the door, offered a smile, followed him down the path, said goodbye as the car drove off, and hurried back to the house. She saw Cadi coming downstairs. Closing her eyes for a moment, she muttered under her breath, 'Please come, David, please come.'

'So you see, he did come, I told you he would.'

Not listening, Lucy replied, 'I was certain it was my husband.' He might be King David, thought Cadi. 'He'll come, don't *worry*. I'll be glad when they've come and gone, Lucy,' and still Lucy wasn't listening.

'I've been disappointed the whole day, not a word, anything might have happened, I mean the car, you never know, dear.'

'Why don't you sit *down*. Relax?'

'Have you any aspirins in the house?'

'Of course,' and Cadi rushed to the dresser, and brought back the bottle. 'There. Two with a cup of tea will help, dear.'

97

The kettle was on the hob, always handy, ever singing. And Lucy drank her tea, swallowed the aspirins.

'Why not lie down for a while, Lucy? I'll see to the men when they come.'

'I'm all right now, dear,' replied Lucy, remembering the night before, the room.

After their tea, they waited for what must come.

Another knock, and Lucy heard it. Unbelievable. And Cadi speaking.

'Mervyn! Well, well, do come in.'

He stood inside the door, glanced at Mrs Stevens, who saw him hand a piece of paper to Cadi.

'What is it?'

'A telegram,' he said.

'For you, Lucy,' Cadi said.

She tore it open, read it, cried at the top of her voice, 'From David. He's coming, and he'll be here tonight, isn't that wonderful, oh dear,' but Lucy was talking to herself for Mervyn and Cadi were already nearing the gate. The telegram trembled in her hand, and she heard the shouts.

'Yes, all right for Monday, Mervyn, so glad, you know the time.'

'Goodnight.'

'Goodnight.'

The door banged.

'Show it me,' said Cadi, and took it from Lucy's hand. '*Coming by car, hope arrive about eleven tonight. Love David.*'

'*I am* glad, Lucy.'

And she watched Lucy cry her relief into her handkerchief. The voice seemed muffled, but she caught the words.

'Everything'll be different now, dear,' said Lucy, and heaved a sigh, but Cadi held back her own, thought only of a weight gone, an end to the wait.

'Does Mr Edwards have to come Monday?' asked Lucy. And nothing was more definite than her sister's '*Yes.*'

'I see. I think I will go upstairs for a little while,' said Lucy, an observation that brought no comment from Cadi, and the next moment it was too late.

'There! Listen.'

They heard the noise in the lane, the voices, heavy steps on the gravel, slow, dragging steps that once or twice appeared to falter. And when Cadi opened the door, Lucy saw a strange face, a man standing in the light.

'Come in, Mr Hughes.'

'Evening,' said Hughes, flung a glance at the visitor.

'My sister,' Cadi said, and then the other man came in.

So that's him, thought Lucy, all curiosity, and she held the man with a long, steady look. She said he was always grinning.

'A moment,' Cadi said, joined Lucy, asked the final question. 'D'you want to go up, dear. Sure?'

'I said no.'

She watched Cadi precede the men upstairs, the box between them. Lucy closed her eyes, listened. 'Which room, Miss Evans?'

'Show you.'

When Lucy opened her eyes, she saw them on the landing, and the last of the box.

'Be a bit awkward coming down,' she heard Hughes say, and then an opening door, clumsy movements within. 'Sure, dear?' asked Cadi.

'I did say, Cadi, *no*, I'd rather not.'

'I suppose you did.'

'That's the man you were telling me about,' Lucy said. 'Yes. *Well?*'

'Said he was always grinning.'

'He isn't now.'

'Looks quite ordinary to me, dear,' said Lucy.

The movements above stairs brought a sigh from Lucy. 'It's sad,' she said.

Cadi went to the foot of the stairs. 'Mr Hughes!' His head came into view.

'Yes, miss?'

'Screw it down,' she said.

'Very well,' he said, and both men vanished, for like a shadow the man behind him was peering down into the kitchen.

'That Mr Edwards is the only person that's called here today.'

'You've forgotten the doctor, dear, he called, too.'

'And Mr Edwards's wife was supposed to be coming to sit for a while, and she never turned up.'

'I was glad just knowing that the Edwardses were *there*,' said Cadi. 'You'd never understand.'

A door closed, then they saw the two men stood at the top of the stairs, whispering to each other, Hughes pointing at the wall. His assistant was staring at Cadi, and Lucy noticed this, but the expression he wore conveyed little or nothing to her. They clumped down, waited by the door, and Cadi joined them.

'Ten o'clock then, miss,' said Hughes. 'The other arrangements are made.'

'Thank you, Mr Hughes.'

'Right. Night, miss.'

'Goodnight.'

Hughes, suddenly remembering, called across, 'Night, madam,' but Lucy did not look at him, and made no reply.

'He must be over fifty,' said Lucy.

'Mr Hughes is older than that, dear.'

'The *other* one.'

'Oh! His name's Twm, and I think I told you. But does it *matter?*'

'I think I will go upstairs for a while,' Lucy said, and got up.

'Do that.'

And when she had gone, Cadi sighed her own relief.

Father's changed both our lives, and he'll never know it. Pity she couldn't have children. I suppose I'll always be sorry about that. Poor Lucy. And tomorrow's Sunday, and the next day is Monday, and after that I'll be alone, and yet I feel a little afraid of it. She thought of one she had never seen, a stranger. Older than Lucy. How old? What did he look like. She glanced at the clock. Not long to wait now. And then Lucy came down again.

'Are you all right, dear?' she asked.

Lucy, who had cried her relief into the pillow, replied that she was.

'Cadi!'

'What, dear?'

'I hate that room.'

'It's only *a room*.'

'I was wondering,' Lucy began, and then paused.

'*I've* been wondering about supper. Toast and eggs. All right?'

Lucy nodded.

'Then let's do it,' replied Cadi, and Lucy followed her out. 'Well, really, Lucy, just fancy that,' and she rushed to the far corner and pulled away a brown blanket, under which had been hidden a small armchair. 'Father's chair,' she said, and she pulled it clear of the wall. 'And I still don't know why I put it there, imagine that. *What* a pity, dear, you could have had it all this time.'

'I remember that chair,' Lucy said.

'Been in the same place for years, and I still don't know why I shifted it. Will you bring in that tray, Lucy,' she continued, then dragged the armchair into the kitchen, put the plain kitchen one back against the wall. 'There!' And then she sat in it.

'I can see him now,' said Lucy, 'sitting there with his pipe, and the paper in his hand.'

'It used to please me just seeing him there, so relaxed.'

'David'll be hungry,' said Lucy.

'I'll manage that,' replied Cadi, and the promptness of it brought slight acid to her sister's tongue.

'You seem to be very good at managing, dear, you never stop talking about it.'

'And I've managed something else,' said Cadi. 'It's about Monday.'

'What about it?'

'Mari Edwards will be coming to see to the stock,' she began, 'and we've arranged everything, and tea'll be ready for us when we get back here.'

The cup went slack in Lucy's hand, and she dropped the spoon.

'I've made plans, too, dear. I thought that when we got back here, we'd drop you here and just go on. Such a long way, and David will be tired, besides I couldn't stay another night here, and I hate the dark.'

Cadi sat back in the chair, pushed away her plate, subjected her sister to a long, penetrating look, and was no longer capable of concealing her anger.

'*What!* You mean to say you're going straight on, and after all the trouble Mari Edwards has gone to, and can't you think of how kind my neighbour is, wanting to come with us. It's really shocked me...

'And another thing,' continued Lucy, her fingers kneading at the cloth's edge.

'There's David, dear. What about him?' '*What* about him?' snapped Cadi.

'He'll be here within the *hour*,' cried Lucy, her voice climbing, and her nerves with it.

'We'll *manage*, Lucy.'

'There you go again.'

'There are things I would have said to you that I'll never say now. Never,' and she leaned across the table. 'Only this morning we both solemnly promised that there would be no more quarrelling. Have you forgotten?'

Lucy shut her eyes against the flush of anger that she saw. 'I should never have come,' she said.

'Perhaps you shouldn't,' replied Cadi, 'and I'll say no more.'

She began a hasty, clumsy clearing of the table, and she hurried away with the loaded tray, which Lucy heard banged down in the back kitchen.

'Cadi!'

No answer.

'*Cadi!*'

There was a candle burning on the table, and Cadi was stood beside it.

'I'm *sorry*,' Lucy said.

Cadi swung round, flung it at her.

'Are you?'

Lucy burst into tears, but Cadi did not move.

The tears come so easily, she thought, but she's selfish; she is selfish.

The hand that reached her arm she shrugged off, and went to the sink, began to wash up.

'Will you wipe?'

'I've been wondering what David will do,' Lucy said.

'So've I.'

'We've done nothing but upset each other since I came,' said Lucy. 'I'm sorry for what I said, Cadi.'

Sorry *again*, thought Cadi.

'Well?' asked Lucy, dreading the reply which might imply that her sister could '*manage*'.

'Time enough when he comes,' and this time she did not shrug off the hand that sought her own.

'David's all I've got, dear.'

'I know that.'

'And I *wish* you'd think again about what I said, Cadi.'

'What did you say?'

'About Averton, dear,' said Lucy.

'What about it?'

The answers arrived in the form of ultimatums.

'I'm still thinking about that,' replied Cadi, and wasn't. 'What on earth are we standing here for?'

'I feel so relieved David was able to use the car,' said Lucy, and she followed Cadi back to the kitchen. 'He'll be hungry, I'm sure.'

'I'm sure he'd get something to eat on the way, dear.'

'He'll still be hungry; it's a long way'.

'I hope *he* won't mind bacon and eggs.'

'He might bring something with him, Cadi. He's a very thoughtful man.'

'You told me,' Cadi said.

She took a tablecloth from the drawer and spread it on the table.

'I've made arrangements,' she said.

'Oh! Have you?'

'Had you something else in mind?'

'I'll leave that to David.'

'He might want to run you to an hotel. I wish you'd done that, Lucy, much more sensible, don't you think? Said so yourself.'

'I wouldn't dream of leaving you on your own, Cadi. You *know* that.'

'If he hadn't come, I'd decided to make you comfortable down here. You did suggest it, Lucy.'

But Lucy wasn't there, and when Cadi looked up, and felt the sudden draught, she saw Lucy standing at the open door, looking out into night, but the darkness held no message.

'Do close *that door*, dear.'

'Not a sound outside, absolutely dead,' said Lucy. To her utter surprise Cadi saw her sister kneel down. 'Cadi!'

She felt hands on her knees, felt them pressing there, then, in a low voice heard Lucy say, 'But you are glad my husband's coming, Cadi, aren't you?'

The gesture was too surprising, and Cadi said nothing. 'For my sake,' whispered Lucy.

The simple *affirmation* moved Cadi. Such faith, such devotion, to one single man.

'Of course I am.'

'I'm glad,' said Lucy, and in an instant was on her feet. 'Listen.'

'I can't hear anything, dear.'

'Is that clock right?'

'Of course it's right. There's nothing out *there,* not yet.'

'I was sure I heard something,' Lucy said, and again she went to the door, stood listening.

'It's a ghostly car, dear, do come and sit down, such a bundle of nerves.'

The real car had just pulled up at The Gunner's Arms, fifteen miles away.

5

David Stevens sat back in the seat. Out of the corner of his eye he detected a light over the door. He then got out, locked the car, and taking a small torch from his pocket he approached the doorway. And the light from his torch told him that this was The Gunner's Arms T. OWEN LICENSEE.

'Ah!'

He went back to the car, shone the torch, inspected the back seat, and what he looked for was still there. One knapsack, and one wreath. Good.

He switched off the torch, opened the door, and walked into the light of a big lamp hanging over the bar counter, and a hum of conversation between three men seated at one of the two tables in the room. The conversation ceased abruptly as he closed the door. He walked up to the counter.

'Good evening,' he said.

The short, swarthy man cleaning the glasses bent over. 'Evening,'

'I'd like a whisky, please,' said David, and leaned heavily on the counter.

The three close-together men now looked up from their beer, watched, studied a stranger. An old man, of average height, almost lost in the huge overcoat and scarf. Looking at his hat, and then at his shoes, they knew he was a man from a town. They saw him turn away, the whisky in his hand, and make for the other table, and passing them, he said quietly, 'Good evening,' and they responded in his own tongue. They watched him make himself comfortable, pull out a pipe and pouch. He put them on the table, and picked up the whisky, took a good sip, and then began to fill the pipe. After which the men at the table forgot he was there, drew closer still, continued their conversation. This came clear to Stevens at the table, and he did not understand a word of it.

Meanwhile Tegid Owen had decided to get himself a glass and join his customers, but held back for a moment or two, looked across at the visitor, suddenly called out, 'Wild night, sir.'

'Yes, isn't it. North wind.'

'Bad on the tops,' Tegid said, and joined his friends at table. And 'bad on the tops' was algebra to the man enjoying his whisky. He looked at his watch, timed it by the clock on the wall. Half-past nine.

'Might make it even earlier,' he thought, hoping everything was okay at Pen y Parc, and that Lu had got over her long journey. Such an awful day for her to have to go. Poor Lu. Quite a shock for her.

Finishing his drink, he raised his head, looked at the men, and at last drew their attention, on which Mr Owen came quickly over. 'Yes, sir?'

'I'd like another. Thank you.'

'Certainly, sir,' said Tegid and took the glass away and refilled it. And once more the faces of the three men turned the stranger's way, and he caught their several glances, and made an effort at smiling. A nice little pub, he thought, and took a long look at the big lamp, and found himself admiring it. He thought it was a beautiful lamp, hanging from a ceiling in a foreign country, and so unlike Rhyl and Prestatyn, where Lu and he went once a year, and liked it very much, and it was so much like England. The proprietor returned with the drink, and to Stevens' surprise joined him at the table.

'We don't get many visitors like you, sir, not at this time of the year. From Liverpool then?'

Offering a smile, Stevens said, 'Cheshire way. Can I offer you anything?'

'Oh! Thank you,' and Tegid got up and got himself a bottle of Border and came back to the table. The men, having forgotten the visitor, now forgot Mr Owen, two of them engaging in a game of dominoes, whilst the third, a much older man, bent forward and studied the game.

'Your health, sir,' said Tegid, and Stevens raised his glass.

'Nice little place you have, it is Mr Owen?'

'That's right.'

'I'd like a bottle to take with me,' said Stevens. Tegid smiled. 'Beer then?'

'No. A bottle of whisky, if you have one.' And Tegid smiled big, and said he had.

'Good.'

'Going far then?'

'Not far,' replied Stevens, and took the conversation no further.

'And now, if you'll excuse me,' said Tegid, rising and picking up his glass, 'and is there anything else?'

109

'I'd like some tobacco if you have it.'

'Shag.'

'Do nicely; bring me two ounces would you, thanks.'

Each time Tegid passed the other table, the men looked up, one smiled and thought what a lucky night for Tegid, who now stopped and watched the latest move, on which all three looked up.

And the thought locked in three heads was, 'Tegid's lucky night', and their eyes followed him to the visitor's table, and the bottle of whisky in his hand.

Stevens had finished his drink. He paid for the bottle and the tobacco, and rose quickly, saying, 'Thanks a lot, I might drop in again on the way home.'

'Welcome, sir.'

'Goodnight.'

'Goodnight,' replied Tegid, and threw wide the door, and smiled the so unexpected customer out. The moment it closed the three men looked down the room.

'Hurrah,' said one.

Tegid came slowly back.

'Come a long way, somewhere in Cheshire, he said.'

'Ah! How about a game?'

'Right. If I only had a customer like that, say one night a week, I'd be laughing all the way home.'

'Ha!'

And then they heard the car moving off, and all of them sat still, listening until it had faded into the distance.

What a wonderful surprise, thought Tegid, and then sat down to his game of dominoes. Looking at the men, he said, 'Mind the clock.' And they all laughed.

A mile away, Stevens had pulled up, and was now studying a map, over the surface of which flashed the little torch. He felt comfortable; he felt relaxed. That welcome break, in a more than welcoming pub, had almost halved the journey. And he hoped he could make it, switched off the torch, and was off again. How quiet everything was. And so many turnings, and lane after lane. Narrowing roads, stiffened hedges, sentinel trees, and the moon riding in and out of billowing clouds. Villages falling asleep as one after another he passed through them. Nothing on the road, nothing in sight, and again he pulled up, and from his overcoat pocket pulled out a flask and from it took a quick nip. The pipe had gone out, and he relit it. 'Ah!'

And off again, and soon the sum total of his day would be locked in his skull. There was nothing he would forget on this long, unexpected journey, and dominant in his mind was the thought of the same journey his wife had made, and so early in the morning. Slow-dragging trains, and two changes on the way.

Didn't want to go, really, but of course she had to. I sensed it the moment I put that telegram in her hand, and he shared the moment and the shock she felt. Poor Lu, and then the quick sigh of resignation, of acceptance. Had to be, and the moment he said it, he automatically increased his speed. 'Turn left at Pig y Bont,' Tegid Owen had said. A nice man. He must remember The Gunner's Arms on their way home. He swerved sharply as he saw the light of a bicycle lamp in his path.

'Phew!' he exclaimed, and pulled up sharply. 'Silly devil, must be blind,' and he got out to examine his own headlights. On again, and now humming as he went. He thought of Lu's sister, younger than her. Cadi, odd name, really, and he imagined what she was like. Wonder what she'll think of me, and smiled to himself. Expect Lu's tongue is well loosened by this time. He thought of their father, and it sent him right back to that big day when he had first met Lu. Farming, she said, in Wales.

A mystery as yet, but he'd see it soon enough. 'Turn left at Pig y Bont,' he said aloud into the warm and comfortable car. And another lane, and this time long, narrowing as it went, but no bends. A nice change. He was miles away now, from his humdrum day at Averton. It was like entering another dimension. He lacked the spirit of adventure and he knew he did. He glanced at his watch, slowed down, pulled down the window, let the fresh air pour in. He put his head out, looked round. No change. Was that a dog barking, waking the world? And then he heard a voice in the distance, and later saw a man coming in his direction, with a swinging lantern in his hand. He stopped dead.

'Good evening,' Stevens said, his head out again, and the man came up. He looked at him. 'How far's Pig y Bont?' he asked.

'Pig y Bont,' replied the man, speaking in English, thinking in Welsh.

'That's right.'

'Ten miles,' the man said.

'Thank you. Looking for a farm called Pen y Parc.'

'Never heard of it. Nasty old night, isn't it.'

'Yes. Well, thank you.'

'Goodnight.'

'Goodnight,' said Stevens, and he listened to the footsteps ringing out on the lonely road. 'First human being I've seen since I left that little pub.'

112

He drove on, humming the same tune, hoped for the best. 'It's like another country altogether,' he told himself.

He hoped his telegram *had* arrived, such an out of the way place, isolated. The thought of the telegram disturbed him, and in a flash he felt uncertain. I hope it has.

And on, and on, and he wondered where it would end. Hope I'm not lost. Stopping again, the torch shining, bent over the map, bending low, peering. And he worried about the two women, thought of them, waiting. A light in the distance, a car approaching, and he alerted, signalled it to stop, got out, hurried to it, just as the window came down.

'Excuse me,' Stevens said, 'am I right for Pig y Bont?'

'You can't miss the bridge,' the woman said, 'about three miles further on.'

'Thank you very much,' and Stevens was highly relieved.

'Not at all. Goodnight.'

'Goodnight,' said Stevens, his face wreathed in a broad smile. At last. And after that bridge I'm really on my way, and for the third time he glanced at his watch. Five minutes to ten. It cheered him up, and he tore away, wearing down the miles. What a relief.

And there it was, the small stone bridge, and he saw beneath it the dark waters. Turn left.

Climbing.

There's a mountain behind them. Can't even see it yet. Glad when it's all over, and the traveller's spirit sagged a little. Out came the flask, and one more, the last sip. 'Ah!' Should make it about half ten, thank God.

Still climbing. Was it to the end of the world? Peering through the windscreen he saw nothing, his eye following the light, and then he pulled up. Had he gone the wrong way? Was the woman right in her directive, uncertainty rising, or was that man wrong? The sudden anxiety was like a weight on him. He got out, stamped his feet. Yes, it was a road. Good.

He got back into the car. There's only one *way*. I am a fool. And up and up, and from road to lane. Then he saw something. A cottage. Immediately he turned the headlights on it, and he saw the window, and the light shining behind it.

Can't be this. This isn't a *farm,* no, must be further on, and once more he got out and walked towards what he saw. There was a white gate. Out came the torch. And he couldn't believe what he read for on it he saw in painted green letters, 'Pen y Parc'.

The surprise shook him, and he stood back a little, turned the torch on the window again.

Farm? Why that's not a farm, never was a farm, good Lord, *I have* seen a farm or two outside Chester. Just a cottage. And once more, just to make sure, he bent over the gate, and the name stared back at him.

This is it.

They had heard the car pull up, and Lucy had literally leapt at the door.

'It's David, Cadi, can't be anybody else, it *must* be him,' opening the door, the light flooding the stone step, and then the gate click and a man coming slowly, uncertainly down the path.

'David!'

'Lucy.'

Cadi saw her rush down, throw her arms round him.

So that's her husband, she thought, and went a little way to meet them, and then they walked into the light, and there was her sister, beaming. Well, well! The traveller's turned up. Poor man. He must be tired.

'Cadi, dear. This is David,' Lucy said, her hand in his, pulling on it.

'How do you do, Mr Stevens,' Cadi said, and gravity in its place.

'I'm glad to meet you, Cadi, that's right, it is Cadi, funny name for a girl,' he said.

Girl, thought Cadi, wanting to smile.

Lucy pushed her husband into the kitchen. What a relief.

'Did you have a worrying journey, David, such an out of the way place. How are you? Sure you must be starved, dear,' and she turned to her sister. 'Cadi, David would love it now,' and she fussed about him, helping him off with his topcoat, the big scarf. 'Here, David,' she said, and literally pushed him into the armchair. 'You look... but after bacon and eggs and a mug of hot tea, you'll feel fine.'

'I'm all right,' he said, and stretched his legs, then, lowering his voice, 'Don't fuss, dear,' and she felt in his tone a ring of reproof.

'A bit cramped in here, Mr Stevens,' Cadi said. 'Come along, Lucy,' and they left him.

Out in the back, Lucy, cutting bread said, 'Well dear, what d'you think?'

'He looks nice.'

'So glad you like him.'

When they came in again, the door was open, and he wasn't there, and then they heard the slam of a car door. He returned carrying a wreath, and a loaded knapsack. Lucy

115

went out again, and Cadi began his supper, and he studied her as she knelt at the fire.

I hadn't really imagined her like that at all, he reflected, much younger than Lu.

'How quiet it is round here,' was the first observation he made.

'We don't get many visitors in these parts,' said Cadi, and shook the frying pan.

He noted the height of the ceiling, inspected the furniture, and finally got up to inspect the clock.

'Nice clock you have there,' he said, and she turned quickly, saying:

'Yes it is, isn't it, belonged to my grandfather. Always glad he brought it with him. It's just like a person in the kitchen.'

Stevens nodded, and went on surveying. What a surprise. Just two up and two down. He must have a look round when it got light.

'Sit in, dear,' cried Lucy, bounding in with the rest of the things.

He noted the crockery, the cutlery, the clean white cloth. Farm, he thought, derisively, and then sat down to table.

The two sisters took up their usual positions, sentinels of the fire. Cadi watched him, waited for her moment, and when he exclaimed, 'Ah, that was good,' joined him at the table.

'And now about the arrangements,' she said, and sat to table.

Lucy was on her feet in an instant. 'Arrangements?'

'We can't all sleep here,' said Cadi.

'What arrangements?' asked David, and took out his pipe, but did not light it.

116

'Lucy hasn't slept very well since she came,' continued Cadi, and she fixed her eye on her, 'so I thought it best, Mr Stevens, if you ran her up to my neighbour's house. It's not far away...'

'Three miles,' corrected Lucy.

'Perhaps Mari Edwards could fix you both up, Mr... and we'll have to be quick about it, since I don't want to keep them up after eleven o'clock.'

'Mind my pipe?' he asked.

'Certainly not,' said Lucy. 'Well, David, dear?'

He was on his feet in a flash, and standing between them, looking from one to the other, sensing a pressure, an anxiety in the air.

'Most thoughtful of you, Cadi,' he said, and looked at his wife. 'But we can't leave you here on your own.'

'I'll be all right,' said Cadi, suddenly wishing them both gone.

'Lucy?'

She looked at her husband. 'Whatever you think best, dear,' she said.

He looked at his watch, and he hadn't expected this. All he wanted was to be quiet, relax after his long journey. 'Well,' he said, and stood facing his wife, who in turn looked at Cadi.

'I don't really mind the room, Cadi,' she said.

'*Please*,' Cadi replied. 'Don't you see how late it is, that I don't want to keep the Edwardses up any longer.'

'Come along, Lucy, get your things. I understand the position. And thank you, Cadi for being so thoughtful about it all. I shan't be long, and I'm not going to leave you here on your own.'

'Lucy needs a good night's sleep. It wasn't very comfortable in my room, was it, dear?'

'Get your things,' said David, and the two women went upstairs.

Extraordinary. The *size* of the place. *Farming* in Wales – really!

'Hurry up,' he called, and Lucy heard it, the first order in the house.

'It's Y Ffridd,' Cadi said, 'straight run all the way, can't miss it.'

'Brought you a little food,' David said, 'just in case,' and he gave her the knapsack, following which he extracted the bottle of whisky from an overcoat pocket, and from his back pocket the flask of brandy, which he put on the table.

'Thank you,' said Cadi, staring at the bottle on the table, he had certainly arrived fortified.

'Shan't be long,' he said, 'don't want to keep you up late.'

'That's all right,' said Cadi, and followed them both out to the car. She had a good look at it when the lights came on. 'Nice.'

'What?' asked Lucy.

'The car, of course.'

'Get in Lu,' said David, and with a wave of the hand dismissed Cadi, and saw to his wife's comfort on the front seat. 'Right.'

'Well,' said Lucy, as he settled into his seat. 'Well what?'

'Nothing, really dear, I'm only sorry you had to do this, and after that long drive you had.'

'Yes, yes but we're all doing the best we can, and I wouldn't dream of leaving your sister on her own at a time like this.'

Lucy remained stubbornly silent as the car moved off, and Cadi shut the heavy green door.

'Sorry you had to come, David,' she said.

The remark astonished, irritated him, and he swung round from the wheel.

'What a thing to say, dear. You asked me to come, and I came, and I had a deal of trouble making arrangements, was lucky to get Penfold to be obliging; he doesn't improve as he gets older.'

'I was thinking of you, dear, you must have been surprised, I'm sure.'

'Well yes, I suppose I was, so small, it's just a cottage, and for the last thirty odd miles I was scouring for a farmhouse.'

'Well, you've seen it now.'

'Indeed I have.'

'Careful, David,' she said, and her husband carefully avoided the looming hedge.

'Who are these people?' he asked.

'Cadi's nearest neighbours, I met them both. Quite nice people, he's sheep. They've a son at school. But they are scattered, aren't they?'

'Strange to me,' he said.

'Of course it is, dear.'

'Not like Rhyl, eh?' and surprised her with the first chuckle of the journey.

'Good of you to bring that food,' she said, a remark that brought no comment from her husband, now bent forward, peering through the windscreen, saying, 'This place, is it a house?'

'I've seen it, dear, quite a big house.'

She leaned in to him. 'I know you're disappointed, David. You are, aren't you?'

He pulled up so abruptly that Lucy was almost propelled from her seat.

'Do be careful, David, we're not in Averton now.'

'No,' he replied, and Lucy said, 'it's much further up.' 'They *are* expecting us?'

'Of course. Cadi made the arrangements, and she's very good at managing things.'

He stopped the car. 'Is something the matter, Lu?'

'Nothing's the matter, and please get on; we can't keep the Edwards people waiting any longer.'

His arrival had heartened, and at the same time, embarrassed her. If only things could have been different, she thought, but then things hardly ever were. I should never have said it, really, recalling her most enthusiastic, and surprising day. Father farms in Wales. Yes, it was silly of me. But it's done now.

'Here we are,' he said, and they turned into a short lane, and there was the house.

'Thank God. What time is it, dear?'

'A quarter to eleven,' he said, and reached over to open the door for her. And as she got out his voice softened, as he said very quietly, 'I'm sure everything's going to work out all right, Lu. At least you'll get a decent night's sleep. You look *tired*.'

'Do I?'

'Come along now,' and took her arm, and went through the gate. He saw a single light in a downstairs room. 'I feel a little embarrassed. They're strangers to me, dear.'

She gave her husband a violent hug, clung to him. 'It's all right. They're Cadi's friends, dear.'

120

'Yes, yes,' he said, then knocked at the door.

The door opened, the tall, slim woman stood in the doorway, and when she spoke, they both felt highly relieved. So welcoming, he thought.

'It's Mr and Mrs Stevens?' enquired Mari, threw wide the door. 'Do come in.'

And they entered the house that was called Y Ffridd.

'How thoughtful of him,' said Cadi, as she opened the knapsack, and took out the things he had brought. Some meat, groceries, a bag of cakes, tea. 'Well!'

She carried them out to the tiny room where the milk always stood. An old man, I never expected that, well, perhaps I should have, let me see, yes, Lucy's sixty-four or -five now. The way time flies. God! Am I relieved, just to see the back of her for a few hours! All that damned fuss about my room; what's *wrong* with it; it was hers long before it was mine, and her thoughts came to a halt. Back in the kitchen she sat by the fire, and thought of the bed she would make up for Mr Stevens. Something nice about him, but really, I never in my life heard anybody dote so much on a person as she does on David. Thank heavens he did turn up, and felt a sudden shock when she thought of the alternative. There's strange. I haven't missed Father a single bit, not since it happened. But it was queer, too, the way it happened, so suddenly. Lucy simply hasn't a clue. I felt numbed, really numbed, even the doctor noticed that. *I couldn't cry.* After he'd gone, I sat on that bed for a whole hour, and I didn't have a single thought in my head. Just like being lost in the dark.

She got up, picked up the whisky bottle and held it to the

light, read the label, put down the bottle. Father would have exploded if he'd seen *that*.

She picked up the flask, with its thick leather cover.

How nice. Wonder what Lucy thinks of *that*. Whisky and brandy in the house, and that big *pipe*.

She knelt down at the dresser, and opened the bottom drawer. From it she took a white cotton sheet, and two blankets. Pillow from upstairs will do, she thought, and placed the heap of bedding on the chair. She then went into the back, and stood at the sink. In it were two modest wreaths. These she picked up, reading the short inscriptions on them. Sympathy from Tybaen, sympathy from Pear Tree Cottage. How nice of them. There's strange again. I feel I've always been here, Ty Coch's just a faraway dream. And why should I go to Averton? What's it to me. Lucy has changed, though she swears she hasn't. And I still find it hard to forgive her, ignoring Father like that, really surprised me. From the very moment she came through the door, from the very look on her face, I knew she hadn't wanted to. Hard to believe somehow. His own *daughter*. H'm! Last night I was thinking about both of us. Perhaps we disappointed him, perhaps he would have preferred sons, somebody to carry on the forge, his own dad was so proud of it. I was thinking of him only the other day, even saw him standing in the forge, looking at Dad, and that hopeful look on his face. Sort of said, 'Keep at it, Madog, keep at it.'

She picked up the flask, held it uncertainly in her hand, slowly turned its top, bent down, smelt it, and then put it to her mouth, tasted it. Like flames in your mouth. How on earth did they drink such stuff?

122

Lucy had butted in, and the words in her ears again. 'You could get something for that old clock, Cadi.'

'Never, never sell that, I love the old thing.' Fancy saying that, it was like she hated it. Yes, what a lot of changes there were in Lucy.

Be nice having my own room back, just going up like I always did, shutting the door. The one place where I was able to read.

Thoughts darted in and out, and one produced a little smile.

Love the way her husband said it, 'Don't fuss, dear,' he said, see her face now, went redder than that fire. Ah well.

I'd best start on that bed, she thought, and picked up the bedding.

The table to the wall, these two chairs, I'd best damp down the fire though. Awful if anything happened. It was at this moment that she heard the car.

'Here he is,' she said aloud, got off her knees, just as the door opened, and there he was.

'There you are, Mr Stevens,' she said.

'Call me David,' he said, and she smiled her acceptance.

'I've got everything ready for you,' Cadi said. 'Do sit down.'

'You don't mind the pipe, Cadi?'

'Not at all,' she replied, and thinking only of an utter stranger sitting in her father's chair.

'Very obliging of your neighbours,' he said, and sent out a cloud of smoke.

'Your first time in this part?'

'Yes. I've never seen so many turns, such lanes,' he said. 'Have you a glass?'

'Of course. I'll get you one.'

'Thank you. Do you...?' he asked, but Cadi shook her head.

'I was right glad of it today,' he said, and he took a gulp at the whisky. 'Coming over here, I thought how extraordinary it was that in all that distance I only met two young people.'

'They've gone,' she said. 'To England, they all go in the end.'

'What a pity.'

'We scarcely notice it now. We're just a small, rather scattered community here.'

'How did Lucy look?' he asked.

'Fine. Just fine, put on a bit of weight, hasn't she?' Smiling, he said:

'Well, she was always a big girl.'

'I was interested how you met.'

'So was I. I expect she told you all about it.'

'She didn't.'

'Really?'

'Told me nothing. Tell me, Mr Stevens, in all that time did she ever mention me?'

He put down the glass, lay back in the armchair. 'Of course, why?'

'So silent, for so long,' said Cadi. 'It did surprise me.'

'But surely she wrote, didn't she?'

'She may have done, and then forgotten to post her letter. Ah well! It doesn't matter, sorry I mentioned it, really.'

But David had got his teeth into the matter, suddenly sat up, leaned forwards, studied her for a moment or two. 'Are you sure, Cadi?'

'Forget it,' Cadi said. 'She was probably too busy to write. Father noticed it, too.'

'The day I first met your sister in Prestatyn she looked lost to me, and I suppose it increased my attraction for her. She hated this place...'

'Obvious to me the moment she came in the door.'

'She never really forgave your father for landing her here,' he said. 'She told me everything, and I can well understand her anger, something ruthless about it, uprooting himself like that, and coming here, of all places.'

'I came,' she said.

'I know. Heard all about it.' He paused suddenly, then blurted out, 'I'm sorry, Cadi, should never have mentioned it. But I'll tell you one thing, Lu does admire you for what you did. All the way here I was asking myself, "What'll she do now, on her own?"'

'I hated it myself when I first saw it, and it may seem strange to you, but every time I looked at my father I was sorry for him. We never had a stricter father. After a while I accepted the change, and in the end I accepted everything, and d'you know the moment I did, I felt all the better for it. I've grown into the place, feel I've always been here, and in spite of everything I've learned to love it. We're all simple, hard-working people in these parts, and we mind our own business.'

She watched him take another dose from the bottle, and for an instant imagined this old man drunk.

'There's always tomorrow,' said David, swallowing the dose. 'Well isn't there, for everybody?'

She seemed to make him wait ages for an answer, and he thought how calm, how final it was. 'We remember yesterday,' she said.

'But I mustn't keep you up a moment longer,' David said,

assumed restlessness, put down the glass, and finding his pipe gone out, now relit it.

'It's all right, Mr Stevens, I like talking to you. Besides it's not every day in the week we get visitors from a town.'

He was earnest, and he was considerate. 'Sure you don't mind? And it's nice to me, just sitting here, and somehow I like the quiet of the place. By the way, I expect Lu asked you if you'd like to come back for a day or two, providing of course that you can make the arrangements. Nice to have you, and Lu'd enjoy showing you round Averton.'

'I said I'd think about it, but making arrangements here is different and you wouldn't understand. And it means getting somebody to see to the stock.' Stock, he thought, and it hadn't registered. 'I told Lucy I'll think about it, Mr Stevens. Just leave it like that for the present.'

'How stupid of me,' he exclaimed. 'Of course, it's the animals; I'm a real townee.'

He laughed, and she liked him laughing.

'I've fixed everything for you, Mr Stevens, and I hope you'll be comfortable. At least it's warm in here. Lucy even talked of going to an hotel, but I told her the only one I knew was forty miles away.'

He got up, stood with his back to the fire, gently rocked on his heels.

'Unthinkable,' he said. 'I'd never have done a thing like that.'

'We get used to everything round here,' she replied.

'But you didn't really think we'd have gone off and left you alone?'

'Lucy likes her comforts,' Cadi said.

He saw her glance at the clock, and got the message, and only now did he seem aware of its heavy tick.

'Thanks for everything, and I've kept you up long enough; you've had quite a day yourself from what Lucy told me.'

When she looked at him with some surprise, he quickly added, 'Lu tells me everything, and I tell her everything, it's like that, we keep nothing from each other. I lived a pretty lonely life myself after Mother died. To me it was a little miracle meeting your sister that day, and we're both very happy, dear,' and Cadi took note of a sudden endearment.

A nice old man, she told herself, and Lucy's lucky; no wonder she can't get back quick enough to Averton.

'Oh, Mr Stevens, I've never even thanked you for the nice things you brought; how thoughtful of you. Poor Lucy simply hates our bacon...'

'Does she now?'

'We ate it because it was there,' said Cadi.

Quite a good looking woman, he thought, but what hands, and it made him remember a conversation with his wife as they hurried on to the Edwardses' house. And how prompt Lu had been with her comment, the moment he mentioned it. 'Father'd never have noticed them, David, even if he'd lived to be a hundred. And I'd be even more surprised if Cadi told me Father had paid her for all the work she's done these years. Which reminds me, she told me an extraordinary thing last night, said Father *forgave* her for being there.'

'*What?*'

'Must have been rambling in his mind, fancy saying such a thing to her.'

'What a thing to say,' he said.

'Here we are, dear,' Lucy said.

And the Edwardses' house looming up, the conversation ended abruptly.

Sitting there, looking at Cadi, he thought about it. Sad, really. 'Right,' he announced, and together they laid out the bedding, first having put both chairs and table back against the wall. How ready she was, how helpful, never a single complaint.

'I've damped down the fire, and left you two candles, handy if the lamp goes out; it's such a nuisance lighting it again.'

'Thank you.'

'Have a good night's rest,' she said.

'Thanks for everything.'

'I'll say goodnight.'

'Goodnight,' David said.

He watched her go, climb stairs, heard a door close. The clock struck. He stood there, suddenly went to the window, heard a draught under the door. He collected his flask, and put it with the candles, then sat down on the pillow, after which he put the pipe in his mouth and the flask in his hand.

Can't believe I'm here, but I am. Terrible if we hadn't come. I thought at one time that I'd never get here. Obvious she won't come back with us for a day or two, would have been a change for her, but no, she said so. I shan't ask her again, nor will Lu. *That's* settled. There's something a bit distant about the woman. Ah well! Bed, and he got up and blew out the lamp, lit a single candle, then settled himself down for the night. How easily pleased some people are.

Lying there, he thought about Monday. Yes, he must talk to Cadi about that in the morning. 'Half past six,' she said, and he thought it a bit too early for him. But this was a new country, and a new day.

What a contrast between the two of them.

Hands behind head, Stevens lay back, and closed his eyes, and he thought of the room above, and the man in it.

I wonder why her father threw up everything like that he asked himself, and in a moment found himself cruising down a narrow lane, pulling up and getting out, staring about him, switching on a torch, and seeing in the near distance a white gate, and walking down a long, uneven path, shining the torch over a doorway, just to make sure. A cottage huddled under a mountain, so shut away, hearing again his own whispered exclamation. 'Anybody coming to live here must be doing it as a penance.'

And he still thought so, and laid no blame on Lu for getting out of it.

Tough luck on Cadi.

He sighed relief into the kitchen, saw his wife rushing down to meet him, arms out, calling his name.

Never saw anybody as relieved as Lu when I came through that door, and he thought how she, coming to the sea for the first time, had altered his whole life.

Would've married a farmer if she hadn't.

A man named Pugh following her about, encouraged by Father. The clock suddenly striking made him think of some great bell, and he sat up, felt about for the flask, and finding it, took a final swig. He then looked at the watch. Two o'clock. He settled himself down, composed for sleep.

The book in her hand fell to the floor with a thud, and Cadi then leaned out and blew out the lamp. She thought of a stranger downstairs, a kind of father figure. She thought of Monday. The little car seemed a quick, unexpected blessing, it would save Mr Hughes having to supply his own. Four of them, Lucy and herself, Mr Stevens, and Mervyn Edwards beside him.

I'm glad Mervyn's coming with us.

The man from Averton came clear, Lucy's thoughtful husband, and she remembered the filled knapsack.

He certainly likes his drop, and the way he smokes!

The clock on the table, with its tiny tick, seemed like a friend. I did the best I could, and thought of the visitor flat on a slate floor, and, listening, it brought home the stillness, above and below. She thought of the letter lying on the table beside her, and the great relief it had afforded her.

I didn't tell Lucy about it, seemed none of her business somehow, but I suppose I must, show it to her in the morning, and thinking of it now, she reached out and picked it up. If it hadn't come? But it had, and suddenly she decided to read it again, and promptly re-lit the lamp, and took it out of the envelope. There were things in it that she hadn't noticed, that now surprised her as she read.

Hendre, Swch y Rhiw. Friday

Dear Miss Evans,

Thank you for your letter. It came as such a surprise. I'm sorry to hear about your father, and please accept my sympathy. A time ago now, and we had completely forgotten him. I hope this letter finds you well, and remember me to your sister Lucy. I expect you're together now. So strange it was to us, your father and sister pulling out like that, all so sudden, and not even a goodbye to anybody.

The letter fell to the bed, and a lump had come into her throat. Fancy that. Remembering it after all those years, and she picked it up, continued reading.

Nothing has changed here, 'cept that your father's forge is gone now, whole thing demolished, and a big house covers the lot. I am well, thank God, and I'm sixty-six next month coming. Now about Mr Phillips. I went over to Maesllan, and I talked to him about it, though to tell you the truth your father's passing didn't appear to surprise him. Naturally he was sorry to hear about it. I talked to him about your suggestion and the answer is that we'd like to help you, so we'll be waiting for you when you arrive, and we'll be glad to see you both again, for old time's sake. I'm afraid Mr Williams is no longer with us, but I did go and see Mr Parry, and I explained everything. Though he's new here, feeling his way around as you might say, I was glad when he said yes, he would come. Only thing, he asked me to specially mention to you is that he hopes you'll arrive on time since he has to be in Penybont by half past one. We may not quite recognize you both, and perhaps you won't know us, but we'll be there.

Yours sincerely, Gareth Roberts.

She put back the letter and threw it on the table. From under her pillow she took out a handkerchief, and wiped her eyes. Then she blew out the lamp, and settled herself for the night.

A nice letter, and again she pondered, and not without dread, on what might have happened if no letter had come. How thoughtful of Mr Roberts.

Outside the wind soughed, a language that she knew. If the sound grew it would swallow up the owl, and that dog that no farmer had as yet been able to catch. Composed for the night, her last thought was of the strange way things happened, an iron rhythm quickly broken, two strangers on her doorstep, and one who was known, and very close, with far to go. And she seemed hardly to have fallen asleep before the dutiful bell was ringing, and another day was calling to her. Dressing, her first thought was of the old man sleeping below. She hoped his slate bed had not been *too* hard for him. Carrying a lighted candle she left the room, and for a moment imagined that her father's footsteps were close behind her, even on the landing, and following her down the stairs. These steps vanished the moment she reached the kitchen, and the sound of snoring came clear to her ears. And a sleeping man did not hear an opening door.

He lay flat on his back, lost to the scene. A closing door, and he still slept. An hour later, Cadi returned and, skirting the still form, carried the filled pails into the back. *That* was done. Returning to the kitchen she knew he was awake.

'Good morning, Mr Stevens.'

A grunt from beneath the blankets, and then a stifled yawn. He sat up. 'Is that you?'

Laughing, she asked him who he thought it might be, and took down the lamp, and lighted it.

'Slept quite well,' said Stevens, and blinked when the light shone down in his face. 'What time is it?' he asked, and felt for his watch.

'A quarter past seven.'

And he finally came clear of the bedclothes.

She showed him where he could wash, and he asked for the knapsack, from which he took his towel and shaving gear. He sounded cheery enough, in spite of his strange bed. Town people were so different. Later, she brought the fire to life, and they sat drinking their tea. Had she been up long? And the tea was lovely. He hoped Lu was all right. And then, 'Of course. It's Sunday, isn't it?'

'I'll give you a good breakfast,' she said, and it brought the smile.

'Hear that wind?'

'I often hear it,' she said. 'And there's no need to go rushing off for Lucy; she'll have breakfast with the Edwardses.'

'Good of them,' and took his second cup. 'What a huge kitchen they have,' he said. 'Been there long?'

'Came over from Maerdy about ten years ago.'

They gathered up the bedding, and neatly folded it, which she put on the dresser. The pillow was following, but she relieved him of it. 'That's upstairs, Mr Stevens.'

'Oh yes,' he said, and thought if she calls me David, it'll be through absent-mindedness. 'By the way, Cadi, there's one or two questions I'd like to ask, if I may.'

'What is it then?'

'About tomorrow. As you know, I'm still sort of getting my bearings. Where will it be?'

'Swch y Rhiw.'

'Say it again,' and he leaned towards her, one hand to his ear, thinking of Melin and Y Ffridd and Pen y Parc, caught up in a new geography. *Very* slowly she spelt it out for him, and his smile was broad.

'Thank you. I'm still learning.' And tentatively, 'How far?'

'About sixty-two miles,' she said, and her casual manner puzzled him even more.

Why hasn't Lu told me? he asked himself, then jerkily, 'Oh, that alters things, doesn't it?'

'Not a thing, Mr Stevens. My father wished to lie with his father, that's all.'

Stevens was full of apologies. He hadn't known, and he *was* sorry.

'She should have told you, shouldn't she?'

'She didn't.'

'Forget it, Mr Stevens.'

He felt awkward, suddenly corrected. He put on coat and hat.

'Don't be long,' she said.

He was glad to get out, loosen stiffened muscles, get into the fresh air, have a brisk walk.

She heard his steps dying into the distance. Poor Mr Stevens seems slightly bewildered this morning, and she started breakfast. I thought he *knew*.

She laid the table. I expect Lucy's enjoying hers, she thought, remembering her violent dislike of fat bacon, and she bent over the fire just as Stevens came bustling in.

'Ready.'

'Thank you,' removing his outdoor things, watching her. 'Always on the go,' and said it aloud as she served him his bacon and eggs. She sat with him, but made no comment; she knew he was enjoying it. Like Lucy, he could only stare at the paucity of her own.

'You don't eat much,' he said, and again there was no reply from her. Inwardly, he still rankled over his wife's silence.

6

'I shan't be long, Cadi,' said Stevens, to which he received a brief nod of acknowledgement, since the remark scarcely registered with her, as she followed him out, watched him hurry down to the car.

'It's only just after eight,' she called after him.

'I know, just having a run round,' he called back.

The car door banged, and the window came down, but immediately went up again, for Cadi had vanished.

And he thought about her as he drove slowly in the direction of the Edwardses' house. Pipe in mouth, comfortable in the seat, and having enjoyed his breakfast, he now fell to ruminating about Lu's sister. Always on the go, he thought. And a bit of a mixture, really. She was kind, considerate, even welcoming, and yet she had her moments of what seemed to him to be complete indifference. Sometimes she listened, and sometimes she was miles away. And then his thoughts turned to Lucy, and he remembered what Cadi had said to him. And he still couldn't believe it. To be silent for all that time, now that was indifference, and a very marked one. *Why* hadn't she written? Pathetic, he thought, Cadi's casual question echoing in his ears. 'Did Lucy ever ask about me, talk about me?' I did mean to talk to her about that, yes... but now I won't.

He was fully aware of cowardice shadowing him, but he had made up his mind. He would forget the whole thing. No rifts. And there was a certain ease about Lucy's simple contentment. Yes, no rift of any kind. Lucy was all, total. That was what mattered, and mattered now. He dug deeper, thought of the tomorrows, remembered his age, and remembered his luck. The history of the last two days would vanish like cloud. And, like his wife, he would be glad to get home. What Cadi did was her concern. His reflections sank from sight, and he felt a certain relief. The practical side of Stevens' nature now took control. He thought of a long journey, and he hoped Lu wouldn't be the victim of car sickness. He thought of the farmer who would accompany them, and he thought of two sisters sat in the back. Arrangements. These might be changed, and he would talk to Cadi about it when they got back. Perhaps he might even discuss the matter with Mr Hughes. And the heavily involved moment blinded him to the fact that he had actually passed Y Ffridd.

'Good Lord!'

He reversed and pulled up at the gate. The first person he saw when the door opened was his wife, there in an instant, as though she had been patiently waiting behind the door.

'There you are, David, dear,' she said, all smiles.

He then saw Mr Edwards for the first time. 'Good morning, Mr Edwards.'

136

'Good morning.'

'Mrs Edwards is upstairs at the moment, dear,' said Lucy, 'and you haven't met Mr Edwards. They've been most kind, David.'

'Thank you, sir,' Stevens said. 'Very obliging of you.'

'Won't you come in, Mr Stevens?'

'I'd rather not,' said Stevens, 'Must get back, I'm afraid, things to do,' and sensing a disappointment, added quickly, 'Do thank your wife.'

Mervyn followed them down to the car. 'That's a help,' he said, and pointed to the Austin.

They all turned when a top window shot up, and Mari Edwards called out 'Good morning, hope you were comfortable, Mrs Stevens.'

Lucy turned, beamed. 'Very, and thank you so much.'

They shook hands with their host, and got into the car. Mervyn waved them away, and Stevens was glad to depart. The top window closed, and Mervyn shut the gate.

Odd pair, he thought, and listened, and looked back as the car turned out of the lane.

The moment they left the lane, Stevens stopped the car. 'Anything the matter, dear?' asked Lucy.

'Nothing.'

'How did you make out, dear?'

'All right.'

'Is something wrong, David?'

She leaned heavily towards him, showed him her concern.

'Why didn't you tell me, Lu?' he said.

'Tell you what, dear?'

'That it wasn't local.'

137

'I thought she told you that.'

'She didn't.'

'How thoughtless of her,' Lucy said.

'Cadi appeared surprised that I didn't know,' he continued, 'you could have told me, dear, it makes things different.'

'Different. What d'you mean?'

He didn't answer, lay back in the seat, stared through the windscreen.

'Were you comfortable?'

'Were you?' he asked.

'I had an excellent night, dear, and such a good breakfast. I expect you know Mr Edwards is coming with us tomorrow.' It sounded like a grunt, but he accepted it. 'I heard,' he said.

'I thought Cadi would have explained everything to you last night.'

'I wouldn't be asking questions if she had, would I?' he replied.

'You're not angry, David, surely?'

'No dear, and we'd best get on, hadn't we?'

'Hope you had a decent breakfast,' said Lucy, and she curled up in the seat, her curiosity aroused, and David's tone of voice was something new to her. What on earth had they been talking about last night?

'Hope you had a proper night's rest. Yesterday *was* a day, wasn't it?' He concentrated on his driving, thought about petrol for tomorrow. A man and a woman passed them by, she in black, and he in a blue suit. Strangers, but he noticed how both stared into the car as it passed.

'I was surprised when Cadi told me,' and her sudden remark irritated him. Why couldn't she leave it alone? But she continued, 'Never expected anything else, and she must have thought me horrible, but I had to say it.'

'Say what?'

'I just thought of all the way back, *there.*'

'You sound disappointed,' he said.

'*What* a thing to say to me,' she snapped back at him.

'Sorry, Lu, I just feel slightly irritated this morning, that's all.'

He felt her hand on his arm, and she warmly stroked it, and said in her gentlest voice 'We mustn't quarrel, dear, must we; remember our little oath?'

He looked hard at her, then smiled, balm for the occasion. 'Just felt I might have been told,' he said, his voice fading away.

'Where did she sleep?'

'Cadi? In her room of course.'

'Were you really comfy, David?'

'Yes.'

'Stop the car, dear,' she said, and he pulled up abruptly, wondering what was coming.

'What next?' he asked himself.

'Is there any need to rush back, dear?' she asked, and dropped down the window. 'I just wondered if we couldn't have a little run round, no, not that way, dear, I thought we might climb a little. The wind's settled, thank God, and it's so quiet, almost peaceful, really.'

'It is Sunday.'

'Well?'

'I don't like leaving your sister on her own,' he said.

And Lucy at once changed course. She said she hadn't much liked going off like that last night, leaving him on his own, and he made her wait for his reply.

'I'll go a little higher,' he said, 'and then I'll get out and have a walk round.'

'Do that.'

They pulled up under a hedge, got out, and he locked the car. He opened a gate and they went into a big field, and she linked arms with him, and they walked on in silence.

'All that mattered to me, Lu, was that you should have a good night. I saw how tired you looked the moment I arrived.'

'You are good, dear,' she said, 'but then you always are.'

'Cadi said you wanted to go to the Edwardses',' he said, and then added rather jerkily, 'I wasn't exactly talking to myself back there.'

'I knew something had upset you, David, knew it.'

'We mustn't go on talking like this.'

'No, dear. What time did Cadi retire?'

Still fishing, he thought, and then very casually, 'Oh, must have been around one o'clock, yes it was. I was amused how surprised she was when I pulled out the bottle, and put it and the flask on the table. Apparently your father never drank anything but tea.'

'A strict teetotaller, dear.'

They reached the end of the field, turned, walked slowly back to the gate.

'What did she talk about, dear?'

'Everything, in fact once she started I thought she'd never stop; I never knew she'd been working in Manchester.'

So she talked to him about that, did she? Seems more confiding to David than to me, thought Lucy, wondering what she had missed. 'She taught there in primary school, think she was there about six months, not sure, fancy her talking about that.'

'Well she did. Incidentally I asked her again if she'd like to come back with us for a day or two, change of atmosphere, but she won't, and I knew the way she said it that I needn't ask her again. Apparently she's going to give the whole house a doing over, and then re-decorate.'

'Just fancy. She seems to have taken a liking to you, dear.'

'She's also made some arrangements with Mr Edwards, and they're going to share the three fields,' he said.

'Well! Indeed,' said Lucy. 'She *was* talkative. What time did she retire again?'

'Must have been around one o'clock.'

'Hope you were comfortable, David.'

'How scattered people are hereabouts,' he said.

'Shall we go back now?' she asked.

'There's something attractive about it,' he said embracing his surroundings with a wild wave of his arm, and then they got back into the car, but he did not immediately set off.

'And another thing, Lu,' he began, 'Cadi asked me if I'd go down and have a talk with Mr Hughes.'

She alerted at once. 'Talk about what?'

'The *arrangements*. Since there'll only be four of us we won't need his car will we?'

'I see, yes, of course, you're quite right, dear. D'you know she hasn't even told me who the two men are.'

'Didn't she tell you she'd written to one or two people that knew your father at Ty Coch?'

'Yes, she did mention a George Roberts and a Frank Phillips; its so long ago. I'm sure they're old, like us. Well?'

'Well nothing, dear, except when we arrive they'll be there.'

'Let's get back,' Lucy said.

Two men in their Sunday best passed them by, but seemed indifferent to the car's occupants.

'Chapel,' Lucy said.

'That's another thing,' David said, and was at once interrupted.

'You seem to know everything, dear.'

'You asked me what we talked about, and I'm telling you,' he said.

'He gave it up.'

'Gave *what* up?'

'Going to *chapel*. Saddened me, David,' she said, 'it really did,' and just a single glance conveyed to him the truth of it. 'Always such a good-living man, and so strict with us all, in some ways it actually shocked me.'

'Cadi gave it up, too,' he said.

'I'm not really interested in what she gave up,' said Lucy, 'and do let's get *on*, dear.'

Cadi heard the car pull up, but went on writing the letter. She finished and read it, and wrote on the envelope 'Lucy', sealed it, and put it away in a drawer just as the door opened, and they came in.

'There you are,' she said.

'We had a little run round,' said David, and then he fussed a bit, helped Lucy with her coat.

'Easily tell it's Sunday,' he said, and removed his own coat and threw it across the back of the chair.

'And how did you get on, dear?' asked Cadi.

'I agree with you about those Edwards people, very helpful they were. After that we had a little run up the mountain road, then got out to have a look round,' and at that moment Cadi realized that something was missing, and rushed out and returned with a tumbler, and some water in a jug.

'There you are Mr Stevens,' she said.

Laughing he asked, 'Sure you won't?' which only made his wife look daggers at him. She got up, saying:

'David does like his drop, don't you dear?'

'Where are you going?' he asked.

'To the bottom of the garden,' she replied, fixed her eye on her sister, saying, 'David tells me you want him to see your Mr Hughes.'

'That's right.'

The door closed. Immediately she went to the dresser, and took out of the drawer the writing pad she had been using, and from between its pages found what she wanted.

There was something almost solemn in her approach, and he was quick to detect it.

'You won't understand a word of this,' she said, opening and holding out the note to him. 'Did Lucy have a good night, Mr Stevens?'

'Slept the night through, she says.'

'I've been thinking all the morning, Mr Stevens, how helpful you've been, and if I may *say* so, your car's a godsend. I *do* hope you don't mind.'

He took the sheet of paper from her, looked at it for a moment or two, and then handed it back, after which she bent over and read to him.

'I see,' was all he could say, and then she put it in an envelope and addressed it to the undertaker. 'He'll understand,' she said.

'D'you want me to go now?' he asked.

Seeing the unfinished whisky at his side, she said, 'When you're ready.'

Lucy returned, then went straight upstairs. 'I'd best get it done,' he said.

'Thank you, Mr Stevens. It's a great help.'

'Not at all.'

Lucy, hearing the closed door, went to the window, and saw her husband hurrying down the path, and as soon as the car had gone she went back to the kitchen.

'Glad you were more comfortable, dear,' Cadi said. Lucy took her usual chair, folded her arms, but made no reply.

'Is there anything you want, Lucy?'

'Nothing.'

'Very good of your husband to do this,' Cadi said, and immediately Lucy turned on her.

'His name's *David*,' she snapped.

'It's still good of him, and I'm grateful, save an awful lot of trouble, dear. You'll understand what I mean, later.'

'I gather you made up your mind, too,' Lucy said.

'I have. It's the only sensible thing to do. I'm staying here, I belong here,' and to drive it fully home, added, 'and nothing will get me out. It took me a long time to make up my mind, but it's made up, and that's an end to it.'

'Nobody's interfering,' said Lucy.

'We've both of us changed, Lucy, and there's nothing more I want.'

'I hear you've come to an arrangement with Mr Edwards,' said Lucy.

'I have.'

'I can't remember a George Roberts,' Lucy continued, 'and as for somebody by the name of Phillips, I'm not sure.'

'Friends of Father's years ago; I suppose Mr Roberts is around seventy now, but Mr Phillips is younger.'

'Wasn't one of them a gamekeeper to the Vaughans before they went off to Canada, Toronto, wasn't it?'

'That's right.'

'Roberts still eludes me, though.'

'The *shepherd*.'

'Of course, yes, fancy me forgetting that. I know you'll think it rather odd of me, dear, but honestly I don't feel much in the mood for meeting anybody back there. You know what they say about people going back to the old place.'

'I don't know. How about a cup of tea?'

'I'll wait till David gets back. And why are you sitting there, Cadi; do come over here. That's better. Tell me, dear, are you *really* happy living here, like this?'

Cadi nodded.

'Oh well. You've made your own life, and I've made mine.' A grave nod of the head from Cadi was followed by a smile. We're strangers now, she thought.

Stevens tore through the village, and then turned left, approached rising ground.

Semi-detached, pebble-dashed, and a big shed alongside it. Good. And there it was. He got out, and walked quickly to the entrance. He heard the sound of somebody humming inside it. He then called: 'Mr Hughes?'

He waited a moment or two, then called again. The humming stopped, and the voice seemed distant: 'Hello! Who's that?'

Stevens walked into the big shed, and saw the man standing under the lamp at a rough-hewn desk. An elderly man wearing dungarees.

'Yes. What is it?'

145

'You are Mr Hughes?'

'Speaking.'

Stevens drew closer. 'Good morning. I've come with a message from Miss Evans,' he said.

'Oh yes?' and Hughes came up to the visitor. 'What can I do for you?' He saw Stevens take out a wallet, and from it a folded sheet of paper that he had been unable to read, and handed it to him. 'May I sit down?'

'Certainly,' said Hughes, 'this way,' and conducted him to the desk and gave him the stool. 'I haven't the name, sir,' he said.

'Stevens.'

'I see.'

He stood under the lamp and slowly unfolded the paper, began to read in a low voice. '*Turn left at Two Gates, then straight on till you reach Plas Newydd, then turn right, and straight on until you reach the forked road, where you turn right again. Thank you. Cadi Evans.*'

'*Hm,*' and Mr Hughes sat down on a bench, the paper in his hand. He did not look at Stevens, but rather in the direction of the road. The visitor waited, quite unaware of the look of astonishment on the undertaker's face.

'She's by-passing the village... well indeed.'

He pocketed the paper, pulled the bench after him and joined Stevens at the desk.

'I understand,' he said.

'Thank you.'

'Yes,' replied Hughes, and inwardly, still astonished. 'Am I holding you up?' asked Stevens.

'Not me. Don't often see a foreign visitor, specially at this time on a Sunday morning,' and for the first time, smiled. 'We have a car,' said Stevens.

'Have you now? Well then?'

'There'll be four of us, Mr Hughes,' Stevens continued, 'so we shan't need a car.'

'I see.'

'Mind my pipe, it's pretty strong shag?'

'Why should I?'

'Did you know Madog Evans, Mr Hughes?'

'Surprised when I heard somebody'd taken that place,' said Hughes, 'been empty a time, I'd say, and the last two people had it couldn't make a go of it. Yes, I did bump into Evans once or twice. Really smiled when I heard about it. Must've seen Madog Evans coming,' and Hughes's face expanded to a smile. 'I think I saw him on two occasions in the village, but not after that. His daughter used to do all the traipsing there. Gave her a lift once or twice with her load, but I rarely get high up these days, 'cept on business. You his brother?'

'I married his eldest daughter,' said Stevens.

'Did you now. Well yes, of course, I did hear something about it at the time; cleared off and left him, I heard. We know everything about everybody in these parts, Mr Stevens, and they didn't think much of the goings on. I always thought of Evans as the odd man out, called him the stranger round here, and he *was* odd in his way, kept himself much to himself. My assistant gave him a bit of a leg up when they first arrived, told me Evans hadn't a clue about anything, I mean regards farming, well, for what it was, miserable bit of soil. Twm Evans actually told his daughter that the best answer to Pen y Parc was dynamite. Never heard where they arrived from, somewhere in the north I'd guess. How secretive can you get? But he did learn, oh yes, they both did, and he wasn't lazy either, by no means, and that Cadi of his, I've never seen a woman work so hard.'

'Used to be a farrier,' Stevens said.

'Did he now? First I've heard of it. Pity he didn't stay at it then. Much wiser if he'd kept his head under the horse's belly. Some folks can't be taught, can they?'

Stevens could only nod, smile again.

'Sorry for Miss Evans though,' and the Hughes smile vanished, the brow furrowed. 'Ah well, that's how it is, sir.'

'There'll be Cadi and my wife, and a neighbour – Mr Edwards – and myself.'

'Understood. You just told me,' Hughes replied. 'And now,' Stevens went on, 'about expenses?'

'What about them?'

As Stevens's hand reached for the wallet again, Hughes studied his visitor, noted the well-cut suit, the splendid top-coat, the shining shoes, the hat.

'You're a stranger, too, sir. Well now, what about the expenses?'

Stevens's hand paused in his pocket, and Hughes quickly added, 'Mr... er...'

'David Stevens.'

'Mr Stevens.'

'How much?'

The undertaker was too surprised to answer, and he looked steadily at the other.

'Let's see now, it'll be 'round sixty miles each way, won't it, well then, I'd say thirty-five... no, around thirty-seven pounds for the whole job. All right?'

'Right.'

148

And to Hughes's great surprise, the wallet came out, and the notes followed, and were slowly counted into his out-spread palm.

'Are you the gentleman from the Border way then, Cheshire, isn't it?'

'Averton.'

'Of course. Just remembered,' Hughes replied, watched the notes pile. 'Thank you, sir,' and he crossed over to the desk and carefully counted them, then sat down and wrote out a receipt, returned and added, 'Just give that to the daughter, sir.'

'Oh, and by the way, Mr Hughes, here's something for your assistant.' The note lay flat in his palm, but Mr Hughes did not know quite what to say.

'Ten o'clock as arranged,' Stevens said, 'and is there any message for Miss Evans?'

The two men walked slowly to the door. Stevens looked up at the sky.

'Doesn't always hold, does it?'

Perplexed, Stevens asked abruptly, 'What?'

'The *weather*.'

Stevens buttoned up his coat, adjusted his hat.

'Yes, there is. Give my thank you to Miss Evans. I admire that woman.'

'There'll be a Mr Phillips and a Mr Roberts waiting on you when you arrive.'

'Right!'

'Good morning.'

'Good morning, Mr Stevens.'

He followed him to the car, opened the door, and Stevens got in, and was quickly waved away by the still-astonished Mr Hughes. Nice gentleman, he thought, and seems to have the stuff, too.

'Sometimes,' said Cadi, 'I used to go off down to the spinney with *Mr Palgrave*, especially when the weather was nice. I always enjoyed that. And...'

'Mr Palgrave?'

'It's a *book*. I *loved* reading there under the trees, and ever since I've always liked looking at the sky through them, it's sort of ribbony-like. And I always came back with something for that vase.'

'Oh that,' exclaimed Lucy, and pointed to a great stone vase, standing on the dresser, and was at once practical. 'You've forgotten to empty it, dear, the leaves are dead.'

'Fancy me not noticing it,' replied Cadi. 'It was so peaceful in that spinney, and you always felt you were really alone.' Lucy who only appeared to have spotted the vase for the first time, now got up to examine it.

'I don't remember that,' she said.

'You wouldn't. I found it in a river bed one day. It didn't even leak. Mervyn Edwards told me that it might be Roman.'

'Fancy that,' said Lucy, who now carried it to the door, took it outside and emptied it.

'David seems a long time, dear,' she said.

'May have gone off somewhere,' said Cadi, and, recalling the filled flask and the bottle, remarked that there were no pubs open in that part on Sundays, a remark that offended Lucy, though she did not show it. And what her sister had been talking about she seemed to grasp in a fugitive way.

'You've quite a few books up there,' said Lucy.

'Yes.'

'I was never one for reading much,' continued Lucy, 'but since I've been in Averton I've read quite a lot.'

The clock striking, Cadi thought of cooking to be done, and at once left the kitchen, and Lucy to her own particular thoughts.

She had only half heard what Cadi had said, concentrated as she was on everything that surrounded her, noting in detail such things as the wallpaper, the low ceiling that was still stained, two plain chairs, and one armchair, the dresser and the clock, and the table that always stood in the centre of the kitchen. She liked the curtains on the window, and remembered that this window was one of the pleasant aspects of the place, in that it faced south. Suddenly, she exclaimed under her breath, 'Well, I never. Fancy me not noticing that,' and surprised herself. 'I knew there was something different here. I wonder what happened to it?'

The sounds out back signified that Cadi was much occupied, and this time she would not go out and offer to help. Instead she got up and stood at the foot of the stairs, climbed two, ran her hand along the thin banister, her eye following it to the top, and she went further up the stairs. She thought it about time something was done with the landing wall. The latched doors were closed. Hearing Cadi come in she came downstairs at once. Cadi gave the fire a vigorous poking, and then put on the pan.

'Stew today,' she said, 'it was good of your husband to bring those few provisions.'

'Don't you have a butcher?'

'Of course we have. Sometimes we have him, and sometimes we don't.'

'Cadi!'

'What?'

'I got the surprise of my life a minute ago and you'd hardly guess what about.'

'Oh yes?'

'The sofa. The sofa's gone.'

Cadi, knelt in front of the fire, dismissed the matter in a flash.

'Oh that,' she said, 'yes, it gave out a year ago, and we took it outside and broke it up. The wood was very handy.'

'What a pity.'

'It was worn *out*, dear.'

'It was old,' Lucy said.

'Hardly need one now,' Cadi said, and then paid some attention to the pan.

'What made you think that David was out searching for a pub, Cadi? I don't quite like your remark, dear.'

Cadi laughed this off. 'Well, it is Sunday, Lucy, and it can be dull to some people, especially those from the town.'

'I still didn't like your remark.'

'Sorry.'

'I still feel it a great pity you couldn't have stayed in Manchester. And you always liked teaching, dear.'

'D'you remember a Mrs Davies from back home, the widow lady whose husband was a solicitor?'

'Olwen Davies?'

'That's right.'

'What about her?'

'I met her whilst I was there.'

'*Really.* Her that had the Wern, and didn't she have a son, Richard, yes, of course, I do remember her now; Richard used to come with his pony to be shod. What about her?'

'I bumped into her in Piccadilly one afternoon. Of all places.'

'Well indeed! Just fancy that. I never knew she'd left the Wern.'

'Sold up years ago. And Richard's a qualified engineer now. That's why she went to Manchester in the first place, to be with him.'

'You do surprise me,' said Lucy. 'But it's still a pity.'

'Don't keep on at it. Besides all I remember of the place is the rain, and crocodiling children through wet streets.'

I shan't pursue the matter, thought Lucy; for some reason she doesn't want to talk about it.

The clock striking, Lucy glanced at her watch.

'He's been out over an hour, Cadi. He said he was coming straight back here.'

'How you worry, Lucy.'

'Wouldn't you? But then, you wouldn't, would you?'

'What on earth d'you mean by that, *Lucy?*'

'Well you don't understand for one thing. He is *my* husband, and a very good one he is, too. And I'll always thank the day I met him.'

'We're not going to start quarrelling again, are we?'

'No, dear, and I know I'm always fussy over David, even touchy if it comes to that, and God knows I wish you were as happy as I feel now.'

'I'm content,' Cadi said.

'But that's not the same as being happy, dear, is it?' Cadi lifted the lid of the pan, examined the contents, then put the pan on the hob.

'Do sit down, Cadi.'

And she sat down.

'I know what you're thinking,' said Cadi.

'What, dear?'

'You tell me.'

'David and I were talking about it only yesterday,' said Lucy.

Cadi said: 'The day I came here, and saw Father, I vowed then that I'd never leave him,' and after a long pause, 'besides there were times when he was special to me, a father always is, especially to a daughter. How could I have married in the circumstance?'

'You should think about it now, dear. You should look in the mirror some time, that's what they're for. You always were attractive, Cadi.'

It touched something in Cadi, and in a flash vanity rose from beneath a hidden stone. 'Yes, there was a man,' she said.

Lucy sat forward in her chair, pressed her hands on Cadi's knees.

'Was there, Cadi, *really?*'

'Remember me telling you about a monthly visitor I have, Miss Jones?'

'The woman that collects for the Missions?'

'That's right. Once, when I'd gone to the Women's Institute Fete with the butter, I met her there, and the man with her.'

'Oh! *Well!*'

'I didn't want to talk about it at *all*.'

'Do you good, Cadi. What happened?'

'Well, we just took a liking to each other, and later we corresponded for a while...'

'What was he like, dear?'

154

'Tall, on the thinnish side; he was a missionary.'

'*Oh.*'

'He was on leave from Africa. The second time I met him was at a Noson Lawen. I liked him a lot. Then suddenly he was gone, his leave over, and back he went. I pictured him moving about amongst the Africans, thousands of miles away. I used to keep the letters until they grew into a little pile, and then I'd have a real feast in my room.' She paused abruptly and looked away from her sister.

I wish I'd never mentioned it at all, thought Lucy. It's really shaken her.

'Don't talk about it any more, Cadi, wish I'd never mentioned it.'

Not listening, Cadi continued. 'Then one day I got a letter, and who d'you think brought it to me?'

'Who?'

'Miss Jones.'

'Why *her?*'

'The last letter he wrote me was care of her, that's why. She said he must have forgotten my address.'

'I hope you didn't believe *that*, dear.'

'I believed everything,' Cadi replied.

'And then?'

'I paid Miss Jones her usual subscription, and I didn't open the letter until she'd gone...'

'Did she...'

'He wasn't coming back, ever, but devoting himself, his whole life, to the cause.'

'Poor Cadi,' and Lucy put an arm round her and hugged her, and felt the body stiff, resistant. 'Poor dear.' And was shocked when Cadi exploded.

'He'd married God Almighty!' Cadi said.

What a terrible thing to say, thought Lucy, though it was with the gentlest concern that she now looked at her sister. *Why* doesn't she come back with us, poor dear, that's what she *wants*. Shall I try again?

'The way you've kept that locked up inside you all this time, dear.'

'There was I, this letter in my hand, and Miss Jones standing by the window looking at me, I always remember that, and all I wanted then was that she should go...'

'You mean she expected you to open it there and then?'

'"Leave me alone," I said, and she left me alone, and I heard the door close.'

'You poor dear. But I am glad you told me, Cadi, I am.'

'I opened it and only read half way through and then threw it in the fire. I'll always be glad I never told Father about it, though at one time it was my firm intention. I was really sad when it happened, for I really liked him. I can feel it in my hand *now*, see the words. He wasn't coming back, he was never coming back, and a ream of explanations and I didn't even read it. What struck him, struck me. And that was the *man*.'

She took her sister's hand, squeezed it hard. 'Now you know.'

'Who *was* he?'

'Came from Pentrebeirdd.'

'What was his name?'

'It doesn't matter.'

David is late, thought Lucy, wondering what had happened. Cadi, bent over the fire, examined the contents of the pan, then turned to Lucy again.

'I *hated* myself,' she said, 'for the wish, for the very thought, for hoping – even *imagining* it, for *wanting* to. *I* could never have told Father that, never.'

'No, dear.'

Cadi suddenly got up and walked to the window. There seemed a casualness in her sister's reply. She'd dragged it out of me, and now cursed herself for ever having mentioned it, something deep inside, anchored, lost, forgotten.

'Cadi!'

Cadi swung round, and with a sort of low scream, her voice rising, exclaimed passionately, 'I don't... want to talk about it *any more.*'

'No, dear, still, I'm glad you told me,' and, following a pause, 'but I still think it awful.'

She then joined her sister at the window.

'Almost mild today,' she said, and opened the door and stood out on the step. 'What on earth's happened to that man of mine, dear?'

'There!'

They both listened.

'False alarm,' said Cadi.

'Thought I heard something,' replied Lucy. Cadi's surprising words had already sunk to the bottom of her mind. A man from Pentrebeirdd seemed suddenly out of another world, and David was too close.

'Are you going to stand out there all day?' asked Cadi.

'I wish David would come.'

Oh, God, Cadi thought.

The door closed. Cadi sat down, but Lucy did not. 'Do sit down, Lucy. He won't get lost.'

So Lucy sat.

The clock struck.

'It's one now,' cried Lucy.

But Cadi made no reply, folded her hands, closed her eyes. They waited.

Stevens talked to himself as he drove away from Y Fraich. And leaving the shed he had caught sight of a man emerging from behind a stack of wood, and presumed it must be Mr Hughes's assistant. Wears a cap on the back of his head. Hardly glanced my way. So here I am driving about in a strange place, and Lucy waiting for me, and her sister giving me a letter in Welsh for Hughes, and all this happening just because an elderly man that shod horses dug up his root on the spur of the moment. He looked at his watch, suddenly thought about petrol, filling up, and something extra for Tuesday. What a long wait it had seemed. That kitchen was even beginning to press down on me. Lucy's right. Wonder how old the place is. Doesn't even have a damp course. No, but then it is old. He turned right and came to the main road. Seeing a man and woman approaching him, he pulled up, and stuck his head out of the window. Was he right for the town?

'Oh yes. Another twenty miles,' the man replied, and Stevens thanked him, and drove on.

The Border, he thought would accommodate him. Can I do it? He immediately put his foot down, and the world began to fly by. It's almost like calculation, he told himself, and heard again the voice of Cadi, the grave, 'Mr Stevens'. Ah well, I'll hear all about it from Lu when we get back. Only been here two days and it seems like a month.

He supposed that people that chose such a way of life really liked it. So she's going to stay on there, and work in with that

Mr Edwards, a nice couple, I must say. He must be at least twenty years older than her. And what a difference between the two places. He laughed to himself, remembering the Prestatyn day. Lu really expanded herself then. *Farm!* Just a little holding, that's all. The traffic increased as he drew nearer the town. He pulled up a big garage, and made certain there would be no shortage on Tuesday. Understand Lu's shock, it is a long way, still, the poor man wants to go home and home he'll go. Funny in a way, once or twice I told myself I might even have liked to meet Lu's father. From the way she's talked to me about him, I'd the feeling he had everything save real affection. Lu's right. Wanted sons.

'Anything else, sir,' enquired the sharp, bright youth, with his head half way through the window.

'That's all, thank you,' and Stevens settled with him. 'Tell me, son, where is the nearest pub round here?'

'On your right, sir, two miles, The Dragon.'

'Much obliged,' he said, dropping a coin into the waiting hand.

'Empty. Well well.'

He took his glass of beer to the furthest table, and sat down. Then he filled the pipe, and as he filled it, took in the whole place.

'Your slack day?' he called to the man behind the counter.

'Generally is, sir, Sunday's blank, really, except for the long distance that pull up here from time to time, cyclists, people like that.'

'Yes, of course,' and Stevens sipped his beer, lit his pipe, relaxed, but not before checking his watch with the pub clock. 'Your clock right?' he asked.

159

'Dead,' replied the proprietor, and vanished behind a blue curtain.

Stevens thought about improvements to the Austin, sensed that even in Wales nobody ate before one o'clock on Sundays, and knew that, barring accidents he'd be back in good time.

Wonder what they've been talking about this morning. They don't give out much, I must say, but Lu'll tell me everything on the way home. I wouldn't know what Cadi could do in a place like Averton, even if she did change her mind and come back with us. Lu wants her to stay, but what could she do? Seemed to know nothing about work, beyond what she bends to at Pen y Parc. Why, of course, Lu says she taught in Manchester for nearly a year. Yes, she might even find something in Averton, after all. The things she told me last night. Just like a man talking to you. And from what she said I thought she must have met herself coming downstairs as she was on her way up. *What* a miserable little room, no wonder Lu couldn't get a decent night. And we'll have to think about tonight, and Monday, yes. Very obliging of those Edwards people, how fortunate for Cadi they're so close. Won't hear a word said against them. See her point. And he had a sudden vision of Cadi in action, a real litany of hard work, that somehow never appeared to cease, and it ran off his tongue. Digging, weeding, milking, looking after poultry, a pig, wielding a scythe, an axe, trimming hedges, ditching, cooking, and those two-mile treks to the village.

Fancy daring to start all over again, at sixty-five, something he knew nothing about, and neither did she. Poor devil. Makes you think. It was time to go, then as he got up a man walked into the pub.

'You there, Tom?'

And Tom appeared immediately.

'I'll have that parcel now,' said the man, 'and is there anything you want brought back tomorrow?'

'Small box at the station. Busy day tomorrow.'

'Always is.'

Tom picked a glass, gave the sign.

'Not now,' the man said. 'In a hurry.'

'Right.'

'See you,' the man said and vanished.

'Your friend sounds a terribly busy man,' remarked Stevens.

'Always is. Market day Mondays, right down the line.'

'Well, good morning,' said Stevens, and hurried back to the car.

Market day tomorrow, could be awkward. How on earth could Cadi have forgotten that, and he visualized the occasional hold-ups, cattle and milk lorries, to say nothing of increased car traffic, and without doubt some hooting on the way. What a thing. Didn't have a clue about it. Must mention this as soon as I get back.

Another look at his watch told him he could easily make it.

Enjoyed the run, wish Lu could have come, but of course she couldn't. Once clear of the main road, he increased his speed.

Eating up the miles, he thought of another distance. Yes, I quite see Lu's point there.

It was five minutes past when they heard the car pull up. 'There he is.'

They finished laying the table, and Cadi was serving the meal when Stevens walked in.

'Here we are again.'

'Just in time,' said Lucy, 'give me your coat, dear, and sit in whilst it's hot,' and Stevens sat down.

'Where did you go?' she asked.

Stevens threw it off before concentrating on his stew. 'Had a run round. Nice morning, too.'

He noted the clean white cloth, and some of the cutlery engaged his interest, and he thought they might have been bought at some local auction. There was a sudden silence, and when he looked up he caught the inquisitive look from his wife.

'What are you thinking of, dear?'

'Me? Nothing, really,' and turned to Cadi. 'Very nice,' he said, and she for her part was only surprised he hadn't produced either flask or bottle.

'I'm not at all sure now whether Mr Edwards *can* come with us.'

'Why,' he asked, and Lucy reinforced it with, 'Yes, why, dear?'

'The dog's back again, a damned nuisance,' Cadi said.

'A dog?'

'An Alsatian, and nobody appears to know who it belongs to. Been worrying sheep again, and Tybaen lost two only a month ago, and Mervyn's worried.'

'Oh! How disappointing for you, dear,' Lucy said.

'I still hope he can come. He's away with the gun this morning.'

'Of course,' said Stevens, pushing away his plate, after which the pipe followed.

Secretly, Lucy felt a slight relief. She had never wanted a stranger at the funeral.

And with her husband's next observation, the dog vanished. He looked at Cadi, but addressed his wife.

'I'd like to take Cadi for a little run, too,' he said. 'Shan't be long. Half an hour.'

'Where, David?' said Lucy, the remark having dropped into her lap with the effect of a small bomb. What was she to do?

'Up the mountain,' he said, 'back in half an hour.'

'But Lucy doesn't like being left alone in the house,' Cadi said. 'And is it all that important, Mr Stevens?'

Why on earth can't she be a little warmer, was the single thought in Lucy's head.

'Why can't you talk here, dear?' she asked.

'It's not what I want to talk about, Lu, it's just that I'd like to give your sister a little run round. We shan't be long, dear, half an hour at most.'

'Oh, very well then,' replied Lucy, and hated saying it.

'Then that's settled.'

Cadi got up, began to clear the table. But Lucy was still worried, and followed her out to the back.

'I wonder what David wants to say to you, dear, that can't be said in that kitchen?'

'How would I know. Did you enjoy the stew?'

'I did.'

'I'd enjoy a little run in that car.'

'I'm not stopping you.'

'But if you're really afraid of being left alone, I won't go.' 'Just go,' replied Lucy, and left her. 'You don't have a Sunday paper, I suppose?'

'Sorry, we never did. There's the local,' Cadi said.

'That'll do.'

'I shan't be long, Mr Stevens,' Cadi said and went straight upstairs. He put on his coat and hat, sat and waited. And

163

when she came down it was the first time he'd seen her in a coat and headscarf.

'Ready.'

'Right then.'

Lucy had not moved from the back, but as soon as the door closed she rushed in, and then to the window, and watched the car go off, wearing an expression as though the little Austin was starting off for a run round the world. She made herself comfortable, and opened the Wednesday local paper.

I used to bring this thing from the village once a week. Nothing in it, really, 'cept auction sales, and local gossip.

The sound of the car moving off rekindled her thoughts. What on earth does he want to talk to her about? Does he have go out for that? All very sudden, and finally she decided to be content with a simpler reason. Yes, well, I wouldn't begrudge her a little run in a car, she is locked up here most of the time. No, I don't want to seem selfish. Still, I just don't like being *alone* here, that's all. Silly maybe, but it's still a fact. And Father upstairs. I hope they won't be *too* long, and she finally concentrated on the peace offerings of the paper in her hand.

'My car journeys are few and far between, Mr Stevens,' said Cadi, sat back in the seat, and occasionally glancing at the man beside her, studying his big, firm hands on the wheel, and the eye never moving from the windscreen, and then had a fleeting glimpse of the house of her nearest neighbour.

'You look as though some mountain air would do you good,' Stevens said, and offered her a smile. 'But there's another reason for my asking you out,' he said. 'And I didn't want to discuss it with Lu there. She can fuss unduly, perhaps you've noticed that,' a remark that got no reply from her save the smile.

She turned to him. 'Well, Mr Stevens, what is it?'

'It's about tomorrow,' he said.

'*Tomorrow?*'

'Yes, Cadi. Didn't you know it's market day?'

'Oh God!' and Cadi lurched forward in her seat. 'Fancy me forgetting *that*, I'm all over the place the last three days, Mr Stevens.'

'Sorry,' he said, 'but I felt I had to tell you.'

'I'm glad you did,' she said, and clapped a hand to her forehead. 'The most important day of the week and it never entered my head. It's almost barmy.'

'It changes things,' he said.

'Yes,' she thought, 'it *does*,' and a little run for some mountain air seemed no longer a part of the picture.

'Hadn't a clue myself,' he said, 'but after I left Mr Hughes I decided to have a run, and I thought too, of stocking up on the essential, petrol, very necessary. After that I dropped into a pub called The Dragon, heard of it?'

She shook her head.

'A man called in whilst I was there, I was the only visitor to the place till he arrived, friend of the licensee, looked like it, and it was whilst they were talking that I suddenly heard the word, "Market". After he'd gone I talked to the proprietor about it, and he then told me it was market day all along the line.'

Cadi bit her lip. 'I should have remembered it. I must be mad. It alters things.'

'I know,' he said.

And she thought of milk lorries, cattle trucks, cars, and Stevens thought of many narrow roads. He stopped the car.

'Would you like to get out here for a little walk?' he asked.

She was almost formal in her reply. 'Very well,' she replied.

Studying her profile as she got out of the car he ruminated. So withdrawn, he thought, and ever since I arrived here I've been thinking of *ways* in, and when she slipped he caught her arm, and they ambled slowly up a long, winding path, and stopped at the big gate.

'I don't want to be out too long,' she said, 'Lucy doesn't like being left in the house by herself.'

'We've only just come out, Cadi.'

'Still...' and she hesitated, and then, 'well, only yesterday when I had to go and see Mr Hughes, she came following after me, leaving Father alone there.'

'I'm sorry about that,' he said, 'and I understand how you feel. What d'you think about Lu?' he asked, 'how d'you find her?' He had to wait for the answer, and for the moment was intrigued by an expression of utter bewilderment on her face. I should never have asked. She doesn't really want to talk to anybody.

'She's changed a lot,' said Cadi, 'but she looks well, she always did, Mr Stevens, and she was always very fond of her comforts. But it's quite a time, and we've both changed.'

'You were glad to see her?' he asked.

'Naturally.'

'She worries about you, Cadi,' he said. Leisurely, he knocked out the pipe, and waited for an answer, but she had turned away from him, and was looking back the way they had come. 'You won't change your mind, Cadi?' he said, and this was the last time he would ask her.

'I can't make plans now,' she said. 'I think we should go back.'

166

She's anchored on something, he told himself, and visitors and enquiries are prohibited. 'Come along then.'

He had a mind to take her arm as they went down this stumbling stretch of ground, but didn't, and they got back into the car. He sat there, hands idly on the wheel, as if hesitant about moving, wondering what she would say, perhaps something abrupt and surprising, but glancing her way he realized she was entirely locked inside herself.

He doesn't understand, he doesn't *know*. *I'll* never forgive her for deserting Father at such a time, it was cruel, and it still is.

'Right,' he announced and they began the journey home. 'It was nice of you both to ask me,' Cadi said, 'but Lucy understands.'

He did not reply, and he did not want to, occupied by other thoughts, and clear in his mind was the coming of night, and he supposed there would be no change. Running Lu to the farm, coming back, making up his bed, watching her go up to her room.

'Here we are.'

They were both surprised to find Lucy sat outside the door, and a big cushion behind her. She waved as they came up, called, 'A nice morning, almost mild, David,' and as Cadi passed her, 'You've lost a few cobwebs, dear,' but Cadi went by without a single word in reply.

'Bring a chair out, David,' said Lucy.

He sat beside her, saying, 'She's gone straight upstairs, dear. I can see you're curious. Well, I took her out because I wanted to talk about tomorrow. It's going to be a bit awkward, and there'll be a lot of traffic on the road, I'm afraid.'

167

'*Well?*'

'Makes the difference, Lu, and I explained it to her. Some sixty odd miles is a long way at funeral pace.'

'Oh dear! It is awkward,' she said.

'I explained that,' he said. 'I didn't want you to be bothered, Lu.'

'How thoughtful, dear.'

Although they did not know this, Cadi was standing at the open window, looking down on them, still surprised that Lucy should elect to sit outside, having noticed how extremely fond she was of the kitchen fire.

'Do explain it, dear,' said Lucy, and looking at her he had half a mind to smile, realizing that she was putting on one of her helpless gestures. 'I don't quite understand.'

'You will in the morning. Surprised me that Cadi had forgotten it. I've never seen her look so angry before, just a momentary lapse of memory. Of course I told her I'd talk to you about it, dear.'

'Quite right.'

'There'll be occasional hold-ups, I'm sure, there'll be cattle trucks behind us wanting to get on to market...'

'Market. Of *course*, dear. Imagine her forgetting such a thing. *Really.*'

'And the odd milk lorry, and there'll be an increase in car traffic.'

'Of course.'

'We could ask Mr Hughes to go ahead on his own, and we could meet him there.'

'But *I'm* thinking of the people that'll be waiting there, dear.'

'Yes yes,' he said, irritably.

'Be bad if we were late, David, I'd feel awful. The last thing I want is keeping two elderly men waiting for us, even the weather might change. Then there's this Mr Parry who'll be at the committal.'

Stevens' head slowly nodded, and he passed a hand across his forehead. 'Tricky, dear.'

'Did you explain it to her?'

'Well, no, I hardly liked to, dear, credit me with some sensibility.'

'Yes, David,' she replied, and very promptly indeed. 'We must talk about it over tea, and get the matter settled. Where is she? She rushed past me without even a glance. She does have her moods.'

'Teatime then,' he replied. 'They don't have Sunday papers here.'

'Surprised you didn't bring one back,' she said. 'God knows, things have been difficult enough,' she continued. 'You've been so good, David, coming over like this. In a sense you're a stranger, dear, and Cadi hasn't helped much, so withdrawn, and looks at me from time to time as though she was determined to be.'

'I think her father meant much to her, Lu,' he said.

'If I hadn't gone away that time Cadi mightn't even be here,' she said.

And he was hesitant in his reply, as he thought, I'm getting involved and I don't want to get involved. I suppose living in such a shut-away place for so long does affect people.

'Let's go in, dear, it's getting rather chilly, shall we?'

'It is a shut-away place, Lu, you must admit it, no wonder you jumped at your chance.' He rose and picked up the chair. 'Living in these kinds of places for a long time can affect some

169

people.' She, too, had risen, cushion under one arm, the chair swinging in the other hand. Suddenly she dropped them both, gripped Stevens' arms, and clutched hard.

'If you ever left me, David,' she said, 'I'd just die.' He was touched by this. 'Do *go in*, dear.' He picked up the chairs and followed after. 'What time is it, David?'

'There's the clock,' he replied.

Looking at him as he sat down, she realized what was missing. The Sunday papers. 'What a pity, dear,' she said.

'Get me a glass,' he said, and she hurried out and got one.

'There! I'm surprised you never brought some papers back, David,' after which she blew her nose most vigorously into her handkerchief. He hoped she hadn't caught a chill. He got himself a drink, asked her if she would like one, 'Warm you up, Lu,' but she was adamant, no, she never drank, none of them drank, and she wouldn't start now.

Cadi, idly going through the books on the shelf, thought, not of them, but about tomorrow, and again she cursed herself for forgetting such an important day. And she wondered what Mr Stevens had in mind. Astonished me, seeing Lucy sat outside the house. She would go down soon and make tea. She heard the talking below, but it conveyed nothing to her.

'I know you like your drop, David, and when you were so late getting back, I guessed you'd propped into a pub somewhere or other. What a good job you did, we must settle the matter when Cadi comes down.'

His reply was direct, and seemed final. 'It's your sister's business,' he said.

170

Cadi came down, and passed through the kitchen without a word, on which Lucy immediately followed her out, leaving her husband to enjoy his whisky and his pipe.

'David told me, dear.'

'He told me, too. Heavens, I felt such *a fool*. Fancy me forgetting.'

'Don't worry. Things will work out right,' said Lucy, and began putting crockery on the tray. 'David!'

'Hello!'

'Put that kettle on, dear.'

'Will do.'

'I wondered why David had asked you out, dear.'

'So did I.'

'And now we know.' Tray in hand, and half way into the kitchen, Lucy stopped dead. 'You have thought about it, Cadi? It is important.'

'Of course it's important, and I've thought about it.'

'Well?'

Lucy laid the table, and Cadi made the tea. 'Tea, dear.'

All three sat down.

'*Well?*' repeated Lucy.

'What's the alternative?' asked Cadi, looking directly at Stevens.

'David and I discussed the matter this morning, dear,' Lucy said.

'I gathered that,' replied Cadi.

And Stevens explained everything, in a tremulous voice, and this surprised Lucy.

'No.'

The cup shook in her hand, and she put it down with a crash. And they knew the answer.

171

'You've both surprised me,' Cadi said, and did not add that the suggestion had truly shocked her. 'I wouldn't dream of such a thing.'

At this moment Stevens hardly knew where to look, and certainly had nothing more to say, and regretted most bitterly ever having mentioned it. He wanted to say he was sorry for ever having made the suggestion, but the practical side of him told him he was right. Glaring at her sister, Cadi said, 'And I'm surprised at *you* Lucy.'

'It was you that made the date, my dear,' Lucy reminded her, on which Stevens himself cut in.

'I'm sure your Mr Hughes knew what day it was, though he made no comment about it.' He looked at Cadi. 'I can't see any difficulty at all, Cadi, heaven knows why I brought it up.'

'Mr Hughes will do what he's told,' said Cadi, and left them abruptly. 'I shan't be long,' she said, and she put on her coat and scarf.

Neither of them spoke until she reached the door.

'Where are you going dear?' asked Lucy.

'I'm going to see the Edwardses,' she replied, and banged the door.

'Well!' exclaimed Stevens, and looked at his wife. 'You see what I mean, David,' Lucy said. 'Afraid I don't, Lu.'

'She hates me, and I wish to God I'd never come here, that's all.'

He sat close beside her, dropped his voice, was at his gentlest. 'Lu, dear, we mustn't go on talking like this, really we mustn't.'

'I meant what I said, dear.'

'Please don't go on,' he replied.

172

'She didn't even ask you to run her up there; it's a long way.'

'She's used to walking, and now, shall we leave it *alone.*'

'Yes, dear.'

'Good.'

And Lucy once more buried herself in the local paper, and Stevens sat silently enjoying his pipe. He thought about to-morrow's awkward moments. He thought of the kindness of the farmer's wife. 'The least we can do when we get back is to stay and have tea here. Mrs Edwards has arranged everything. I know you wanted to go straight on after dropping your sister, and I know you'll understand that's the last thing I'd dream of.'

'Yes, David.'

'In the circumstances we couldn't have gone to an hotel. And the weather hasn't helped.'

'No, dear,' and Lucy turned a page, but not a word of it was she reading.

'Thank God for the car,' said Stevens.

'Yes, dear,' and Lucy turned another page. 'David.'

But to her astonishment her husband had fallen asleep in the chair.

7

The door was closed, and for some reason, so were the windows. There were two women upstairs, and two men downstairs, and whilst waiting for what must come, they talked. Lucy was dressed and ready, and, unusual for her, she was watching her sister sat at the dressing-table, looking into the mirror. In her hand she held a blue tube, from which she squeezed something white, and slowly dabbed her cheeks. And it seemed strange to Lucy that Cadi should be so indifferent about herself, as a woman, and on the spur of the moment she got up and stood behind her, saying, 'Too much, Cadi, really it is. What is it anyway?'

'I got it from Mrs Hopkins, Central Stores,' and she turned and looked up at her sister. 'I do get around, you know, and I always bring something back from the market.'

'You've still got too much on, dear, noticeable at once.'

She whipped a handkerchief from her pocket, and attended to the matter. 'There! That's better,' and she returned to the bed. She thought it a welcome change to see her sister actually wearing a white blouse, and a black serge skirt, and from some odd corner of the room she had even managed to find and polish a pair of shoes. 'Such a relief to see you wearing something different, Cadi. Do you always go about in the same old things?'

Cadi, now occupied with her hair, made Lucy wait for an answer.

'You must think me pretty dumb, dear,' she said. 'But you do look nice, Cadi, and it pleases me.'

Finished with the mirror she came and sat on the bed beside Lucy. 'Oh,' exclaimed Cadi, 'here's something I meant to show you, but quite forgot,' and took a letter from her skirt pocket and gave it to her.

'What is it?'

'Just a letter. From Mr Roberts.'

'*The* Mr Roberts?'

'That's right. I never expected to get an answer, and that was the most worrying thing of all, Lucy, you know what I mean?'

'Yes, dear, I do,' and she pored over what Mr Roberts had to say.

'What a relief for you, dear,' she said. 'But what a thing to say,' and she read aloud the single line. 'We had quite forgotten him.'

'I attached no importance to it at all. The fact that they are both still there was all that mattered. But poor Mr Williams isn't, and I felt sorry about that. You remember him, Lucy?'

'Yes, dear, I do. Apart from that one line it's quite a nice letter. Fancy the forge being demolished. House now where it used to stand.'

175

'What pleased me most about it was his thoughtfulness, remembering to go and see their Mr Parry.'

'Yes, dear, it was. It will save a lot of worry. And you were quite right. I still hope neither of them recognise me, I really do, I feel rather ashamed about the whole thing. But it wasn't my fault, was it?'

'No, dear. But I am glad to carry out Father's wishes.'

'Of course. Tell me, do you have to drag out that churn every day by yourself?'

'Oh that. No, the driver always comes in and takes it away for me. Mervyn will help me with it before we set off. They generally collect by eleven. Nothing to worry about there.'

And Lucy thought to herself, She's always so *right*, so good at managing, and wanted to add, but a little weakness might do you good, weak like David and I are, and you seem to have forgotten his name. She was quite unprepared for Cadi's next question.

'What do you do with yourself all day at Averton, Lucy?'

'Me? Why I help David of course, what a silly question to ask.'

'You mean you work in the Post Office with him?'

'Of course. It's not just a Post Office, dear, we sell lots of things.'

'Such as?'

'Well, newspapers, tobacco and cigarettes, and other things.'

'Oh. I didn't know it was a Sub Post Office.'

'Well it is, and you don't listen to half the things I say. You're so tied up inside yourself.'

'Fancy. You are kept busy,' said Cadi.

'Cadi, dear?'

176

'What?'

'Have you got something against my husband?'

'*Why* should I have, dear?'

'You positively refuse to call him by his Christian name. If you really got to know him, he's a very nice man.'

'I'd never seen him in my life until he came here.'

'What's that got to do with it, dear, he just wants to be friendly.'

'I just felt shy, that's all.'

'Silly.'

'*I mean* it.'

'I was surprised when you threw everything into the fire yesterday, such a lot of papers, letters, and things.'

'I suddenly got sick looking at it.'

'I hope you didn't throw the money away, too.'

'It reminds me to give you your share of it before you go.'

'I don't need it, dear.'

'I'll still give it you,' said Cadi.

Noble now, thought Lucy.

'Another half hour and then we're off,' Cadi said, and got up and once more studied herself in the mirror.

'Can you hear the talking down there?' Lucy said.

Stevens talked about Averton, his work, whilst Mervyn Edwards, with occasional glances through the window, talked about sheep, about Cadi and her father, and finally the weather. Coming down in the car with Stevens and his wife, he had been quick to notice the flurry of snow coming down from the mountain.

'I hope it holds,' he said, thinking of sheep, and not of a forthcoming journey to see a stranger home.

'D'you think there'll be many hold-ups on the way, Mr Edwards?'

'No more than is usual on a market day.'

'Quite a distance,' said Stevens.

''Tis rather.'

'Nice of you to come.'

'Cadi's practically family with us, Mr Stevens.'

'Singing your praises from the day I got here.'

And it brought a quick smile from the tall, lean, rather quiet man, whose long legs sprawled across the floor, and who continually twiddled his fingers, and the matter of snow never absent from his mind.

'You're mainly sheep, I gather,' Stevens remarked.

'Sheep country,' replied Mervyn. 'Little you could call farming in these parts. If you want *that*, you take a peep over the Shropshire border.'

'D'you really think Cadi'll stay on here now, all alone?'

'H'm. Cadi will do what she wants to do, Mr Stevens. She's like that.'

'Had rather a time of it the last few months,' Stevens said, 'with her father.'

'She was very fond of him, in spite of everything. And none of us is perfect.'

Stevens nodded. Should he diverge? It had sounded to him like a faint reproof.

'My wife thinks she ought to marry, Mr Stevens, and she's still a very attractive woman.'

'I doubt she'll marry.'

'Oh?'

'Yes, I do.'

Stevens glanced at his watch. 'Soon be time.'

Mervyn appeared not to have heard him, and was at this moment congratulating himself on not having to sit amidst clouds of tobacco smoke. He had twice refused a fill from Stevens, who appeared to have forgotten that he didn't smoke, and had said so, twice.

'Would you like to sit up front, Mr Edwards?'

'Whatever's convenient to you,' replied Mervyn.

And when he abruptly left him, and went to the door, he knew what was on the sheep man's mind. A blast of air shot through as Mr Edwards opened the door to a real wild dance of snowflakes, and Stevens saw him slowly shake his head. If it gets worse, well, he mightn't even come, he thought, and he joined him at the door.

'Can you hear anything?' asked Mervyn.

Listening, Stevens heard the sound in the distance.

'I can. It's them,' he said, and immediately he went to the foot of the stairs, calling, 'They're coming, Lu.'

'They're coming, dear,' Lucy said. 'Are you ready?'

Cadi took a black coat off the hook and put it on. 'My gloves,' and she hurriedly collected them. 'Right,' she said, and preceded her sister downstairs. The sound of wheels came clearer to their ears.

'There you are, dear,' said Stevens.

'Here we are,' replied Lucy, and the relief in her voice she did not deny to her husband.

Mervyn, still stood outside the door, looking skywards, lowered his head, and got a clear view of Mr Hughes's ancient vehicle as it turned out of the lane. 'Here we are,' he said, and he turned to Cadi. 'And you ladies best sit and wait.'

And a whisper in Stevens' ear. 'You'll lend a hand, Mr Stevens?'

179

'Certainly.'

'Good.'

Looking at Lucy and Cadi seated there, he was quick to note the same expression on the women's faces, as though they were neither concerned or caught up in a solemn moment. And he remembered this every step of the way to Penybont.

'Just like it wasn't happening at all,' he thought, and then he saw Mr Hughes, followed by Twm Pugh, coming slowly down the path. He turned to Cadi. 'Cadi! Mr Hughes,' he said.

She leapt to her feet and hurried to the door to meet him. His assistant stood rather shyly in the background. She noted Mr Hughes's black serge suit, and the bowler in his hand.

'Morning, Miss Evans.'

'Good morning,' and she turned to her sister. 'I'm sure David will help,' she said, but Lucy was too astonished to hear her husband called David, and blurted out, 'Yes, of course, dear. David!'

And she watched the four men go slowly up the stairs. 'You've seen what's happening outside,' said Cadi. 'I have.'

'Mervyn thinks it'll clear up. Hope so. Awful if it didn't, as he might have to go back. Always a worry this time of the year.'

'I do understand, dear,' replied Lucy, still listening to heavy, clumsy movements upstairs, and the moment she saw them coming down she turned her back on it, though Cadi herself got up and stood watching them by the open door.

'Easy,' Hughes said, 'easy, Mr Stevens.'

'Sorry.'

And the four men moved slowly, carefully through the narrow doorway.

'Are you ready?'

'Of course I'm ready,' Lucy said, and they stood outside the door. The moment the operation was complete Cadi called to Mervyn, and he came hurrying back.

Together they took the churn down and Mervyn lifted it onto the small platform. Stevens stood waiting by the open door of the car.

'Don't you even lock the door, dear?' enquired Lucy, after she had closed it.

'No.'

There was almost a tiredness in Stevens' voice as he said, 'Come along, Lu,' saw her into the car, and then waited for Cadi who had gone ahead to speak to the waiting Mr Hughes.

A child covered in snowflakes, and school-bound, stood staring through the bars of a big gate, and watched. And he knew them all save one that walked with the men, and the tall, heavily built woman walking beside Cadi Evans. As Hughes and Twm Pugh edged through the gate, he wondered who the man was wearing a big grey overcoat and *grey* hat, his eye following them until he finally heard the sound and saw the man from Y Fraich engage in conversation with his assistant. Only once before had he heard that sound. He saw Cadi for the first time, dressed in black. She stood talking to Mr Hughes, who also wore a black overcoat, a bowler swinging in his hand.

'Yes, Miss Evans?'

'Turn right at Penybont,' she said, and walked quickly back to the car, and getting in she was quick to note an expression of impatience on the face of the man from Averton. He saw

181

them both comfortable, Cadi closed the door, and Stevens opened it again, and banged it hard. He then got in beside Mr Edwards from Y Ffridd. The engine purred. He dropped the window, looked out, saw Mr Hughes wave.

'Right.'

And they moved off.

The watching child had forgotten the time, and the school to which he was going, still stood, and staring as the cortege turned into the lane. After which he climbed the gate and ran fast to his school. Once, he stopped to look back, but they had vanished from sight, the lane deserted.

Cadi sat stiff and upright, as though she could not relax, but Lucy was quite settled and comfortable. When Stevens looked back at them, saying, 'All right back there?' he met an expression that seemed to say, Do Not Disturb.

Stevens, dropping his voice, turned to Edwards, and again mentioned the weather. 'I can't think it will hold,' he said.

'Hope it does.'

The man from Y Ffridd was more relaxed, comfortable. He hoped the man at the wheel, who would soon be occupied with increasing traffic, might forget the pipe in his pocket. Looking ahead he saw Hughes take a sharp turn left, and this surprised him, and was on the point of speaking, then decided to remain silent, looked back at the two sisters. Seeing their stillness, he was touched, and felt sorry for them. From time to time he glanced at Stevens, his eye so fixed on the road ahead, and the tense expression suggested Mr Stevens to be in deep thought. Stevens twiddled his fingers, and watched the snowflakes dance. The rhythm of the car came clearer to his ears the moment he closed his eyes. He thought about Cadi, and the conversation he had had with his wife the night before.

'You'll bring her back for the night, Mervyn,' she said.

'I will.'

'Wouldn't dream of her being alone on that night. Somehow I can't see her staying on now, Mervyn.'

'She will.'

'I must talk to her,' Mari said. 'She's never been quite the same since that affair with the missionary man.'

'Davies?'

'Who else?'

'Hardly an affair.'

Mari had laughed outright, and he could hear her now. 'Women,' he thought.

'We'll wait and see then,' Mervyn said.

'She should marry and settle down, Mervyn, only sensible thing.'

When the car suddenly braked his thoughts scattered, and this disturbance made him look round again at the two sisters. They had not spoken a single word since leaving the house. Cadi had never moved, but Lucy was now rather sprawled in her seat. Meanwhile, the practical man at the wheel was asking himself if this was the beginning. He had pulled up in a narrow lane, and now saw a big van start to reverse until it reached the entrance to a farm, into which the driver backed it, jumped out, and signalled the cortege to come on. He turned to Stevens.

'Market day,' he said, and started off again.

'You'll get the main road in half an hour,' said Mervyn, encouragingly.

'Hope so,' came the clipped reply, his eye fixed on the

green car in his mirror, which to his surprise, hadn't even hooted. 'Fancy Cadi forgetting that.'

'Cadi's mind is much occupied these days,' replied Mervyn. Stevens turned quickly, one hand in his pocket, saying, 'You don't mind,' and out came the pipe.

'I don't mind, Mr Stevens,' came the reply, as the offending instrument was quickly lighted. He had wondered when this tenseness would go, quite unaware that the driver was still partly lost in what he called, 'an extraordinary morning'. Waking so early, and for the first time experiencing the real feel of the floor on which he lay. And worse still the fire had gone out. Hurriedly dressing, and lighting it again, and greatly relieved at its coming back to life before Cadi came down. Stranger still, she had not even said good morning, but had left the house with two white pails.

I felt so awkward, so useless there. A quick wash and change in the back, making tea. Cadi returning and passing him without a word. A hurried breakfast, and then she again vanished, only to return ten minutes later, and he saw her changed dress, heard her say, 'You'd best get off, Mr Stevens.'

Collecting his wife and Mr Edwards. And later, that trouble upstairs the moment Hughes and his assistant arrived.

Ah well! And no real worries yet, thank God, and he little realized that he had practically reached the main road. Traffic seemed to thicken in an instant, and then he saw a cattle lorry easing its way out of another lane.

'You'll be all right now, Mr Stevens,' said Mervyn.

'Expected this,' said Stevens. 'Actually my wife and I were sure it would be local.'

'We were just as surprised as you,' replied Mervyn.

Stevens hugged the side of the road as the milk lorry came by. 'You all right back there, Lu?'

'We're all right, dear,' called Lucy, whose ear was still clinging to those whisperings up front, and she wished she knew what the two men had been talking about. Turning to her sister she again noticed with relief that Cadi's hands were safely hidden inside those black gloves. Such a pity, she thought. Almost as if she didn't *care*. And she, too, offered encouragement. 'Shan't be long now, dear.'

Cadi knew, but somehow the words would not come, and she still sat in the same position, her lips pursed, her eye darting to the window, and secretly praying that the snow would cease.

'This your first time in Wales?' asked Mervyn.

'In these parts, yes. The only two places my wife and I have visited are on the north Wales coast.'

'Rhyl?' asked Mervyn, almost mechanically.

'Yes, but mostly Prestatyn. We go there every year. Very nice place. Indeed, I'm planning to go there for good when I retire.'

'*Are* you?'

'Oh yes.'

And Stevens felt more relaxed, and for the first time, more comfortable during the long drive, and he now turned right, and once more was clear of the main road. Traffic had thinned out, and for the next two miles he had the road to himself.

'What's the matter?' called Cadi, leaning over Stevens' seat.

'Nothing at all,' he replied, as he dropped the window,

knocked out the pipe, put his foot down, and caught up with Mr Hughes.

Up front, both he and Twm had been more voluble. 'Notice we by-passed the village,' said Hughes. 'Well, yes indeed. I did!'

'Sent me a note by the foreigner.'

'Did she?'

'I just been thinking,' continued Hughes, 'I mean how lucky you were for that lot when they turned up here out of the blue those years ago. Isn' it?'

And again Twm Pugh nodded. The words were there, deep down, and they were sorting themselves out.

'Didn't know a thing about anything,' Hughes said.

'Tybaen helped,' said Twm, 'with the plough, I mean.'

'Funny, the way he gave up everything like that, and she had to do the lot.'

'Ah! She was very nice, Mr Hughes.'

'Course she was,' and Hughes looked hard at his handy man, fifty-one years of age now, one who had never anchored anywhere.

'Funny time it was, well no, not funny, kind of odd, really. Once I was coming through the village, was on my way up to old Jenkins's place, remember her Pansy, I expect?'

He did.

'Pulled up alongside Cadi Evans, carrying a load, so I picked it up and ran her home. Such a smile I got. I was so obliging, she says. When the coal came she carried it across a field on her back.'

'Did she now? Never heard about that, and I hear many and many a thing, Twm. You know that man only hit the village about three times, all the while he was there. No wonder they christened Madog Evans the Stranger. Only this morning heard he'd had a forge, somewhere north, I reckon.'

He kept his eye on the mirror, watched a big van behind him.

'What did you think of the foreigner, Twm?'

'Who?'

'Him that married Cadi's sister; have you ever seen such a big woman?' And Twm said, yes, he had. Hughes leaned in close. 'D'you know what?'

'What?'

'Everything might have been different for you, if you'd married her.'

'Cadi Evans?'

'Who else?'

'Ah...' Twm replied, and Hughes saw him smile, an odd look in his eye.

'That would have been a go of it, and you needn't have bothered even looking at her father.'

With a fierce whisper, Twm, said, 'Would have made it good.'

'Course you would.'

'He worked hard though.'

'Course he did, wrong way, I reckon, but she learned to pick up the ropes.'

'Watch out, Mr Hughes,' cried Twm, and Hughes watched out, and glared angrily as a big grey car shot by. 'Can't be far now,' Twm said.

'Ten by the map,' replied Hughes.

Stevens' hands were tight on the wheel, but his thoughts were elsewhere, and Cadi was talking to him. 'I didn't want to bother Lucy,' she said.

'But why, she would have helped.'

'I had to make my own arrangements, and make them quickly. There's nothing for either of you to worry about, the whole thing was quite simple.'

'Yes, yes.'

'Lucy didn't like the idea of coming back here,' said Cadi, and she then told him the details, and mentioned the three men who would be waiting for them inside the gate. 'Doubt if she'd even remember them. Friends of Father's, a bit younger than him. And Mr Parry is the minister, and he sounds helpful; he understood.'

'Did he know your father?'

'No.'

She was right behind him, he could feel her breath on his neck, and he felt like a trespasser.

'Was I relieved when that letter came, it's a long time ago.'

'It is indeed,' replied Stevens.

This short conversation still irritated him. Shutting Lu out, that's what, been like that ever since I came here. Actually called me David this morning, lucky me. He heard the movement, knew she was back beside his wife.

'Ah,' exclaimed Mervyn, seeing a signpost in the distance.

'You all right, Lu?' and Stevens glanced back once again. Lucy smiled, and Cadi said, 'Yes'.

Hardly uttered a word between them since the journey began, he thought, and felt both the weight and length of their silence.

'Looks like we're here,' he said, offered Edwards a quick smile, and his wife's quick sigh had not escaped him. 'This is it,' and he saw the gate in the distance, now open, and Hughes gradually drawing ahead.

'Best wait till he gets through,' said Mervyn.

'Of course.'

Cadi pulled down the window, put her head out, saw the gate, and inside it the two waiting men.

'So strange, Cadi, after all that time,' said Lucy.

'Nobody'll know you.'

The sudden change in her sister quite surprised her. She looked pale, drawn. She's feeling it now.

Stevens stopped the car, sat back, watched Hughes manoeuvre through the gate, and he caught a glimpse of rising ground, and in the distance a church.

'Barely inches to spare,' said Mervyn.

And Stevens moved on, a little way up the hill, pulled up at the grass verge. The snow had ceased, but the whole scene had its thin layer of white, and Stevens thought it even gave a little colour to its surroundings. He got out, and Mervyn followed him. Hughes had gone half way up the hill, and then stopped. Cadi and Lucy left the car, and as they came through the gate she saw one of the two men approaching her, and immediately Lucy lowered her head, and clung on to her sister's arm.

'It's Mr Roberts, isn't it?'

'It is. How are you, Miss Evans?'

'I'm all right,' replied Cadi. 'This is my sister, Lucy,' she added. Lucy didn't know where to look, and she had not forgotten the letter Mr Roberts had written, and the line in it that had made her feel so uncomfortable.

'How do you do,' said Roberts.

And she shook hands with him.

Cadi felt touched by the courtesy of these two elderly men. 'It was good of you, Mr Roberts, and you too, Mr Phillips.

189

What a long time it seems. But neither of you have changed much, I must say.' They smiled at the compliment.

'Your driver seems to be hailing you,' said Mr Phillips, and both women turned, and saw Stevens frantically waving, and as Cadi said 'Excuse me', Lucy rushed off towards her husband.

'I wouldn't have known Lucy,' said Mr Roberts, 'quite different now.'

The silence of the last five minutes had hemmed Stevens in, and the moment his wife joined him, he exclaimed, 'This is a mixture.'

'You'd best go, dear,' she said, 'can't you see Mr Hughes waving to you.'

Mervyn had already gone ahead, and was now standing at the back of the hearse in earnest conversation with its driver. 'Go back to Cadi, dear,' Stevens said, and hurried off up the hill. She could see her sister still talking to the two men. They hadn't appeared to recognize her at all, and she felt highly relieved. It was then that she saw for the first time a man at the top of the hill. Was that Mr Parry? He seemed to be walking to and fro, as if impatiently waiting. Cadi was stood alone, and she watched two elderly men hurrying off to join her husband and the man from Y Ffridd. How extraordinary, she thought. Well, she's done what he asked. Thank God for that, but that journey, and her thoughts leapt to the one that would take them home. An unnerving experience, and the orderly, contented Averton days seemed even further away. She joined her sister.

'And hurry, Lucy,' said Cadi.

'Sure you're all right, Cadi?'

'I'm all right,' replied Cadi, and felt Lucy's hand slip through her arm.

'It won't be long now, dear.'

But Cadi was no longer listening, only seeing, as four men carried her father further up the hill.

'Hurry,' she said, and they hurried.

The pacing man stood still, and as they drew nearer, Cadi felt his eye upon her, and whispered to Lucy, 'That's the new minister here, dear, Mr Parry. D'you remember Mr Williams?'

'Not now, not now,' replied Lucy, and suddenly they were there, and at this moment parted company. Cadi hurried round to where Mr Parry was waiting, and was at once apologetic, and thanked him for his kindness.

'It was the traffic, Mr Parry,' she said, 'we're sorry about it.' He made no reply, but when he looked at her she realized a sympathy in his expression, a benevolent moment, and she knew she would always remember his kindness. The four men moved, and she watched her father go.

'There's no need for us to wait,' Hughes said, and he climbed into his seat, and Twm Pugh followed.

'It was very strange, Mr Hughes, wasn't it?'

'Some things are. Oh, and by the way, I've got something for you, Twm,' and he took out a wallet and from it a pound note which he handed to his assistant.

'From the English gentleman,' said Hughes. 'Oh yes.'

'Yes. Take it,' and he was no stranger to the wide grin he received.

'Ta. We're going back now then?'

'That's it. Such a narrow path up here, and the gate's not much better. We'll soon be home.'

It was at that moment he saw the figure of a woman running down the hill.

'Now what?' and he waited.

'It's Miss Evans,' he said.

'Oh yes, better wait then.'

It was a breathless Cadi that arrived, and called out in a shaky voice, 'Mr Hughes?'

'What is it then, miss?' and he climbed down and went to her. 'You're quite breathless,' he said.

'It's about the settlement, Mr Hughes.'

'What settlement?' he asked.

'There's only one settlement. Sorry I forgot all about it.'

'No need to be sorry, Miss Evans. It's all over and done with. The gentleman who brought me those directions settled with me that morning. It's me as should have told you, miss. Nothing to worry about.'

'Mr Stevens?'

'That's right, miss.'

'He never mentioned it at all,' she said, and he sensed a sudden anger.

'I shouldn't worry, Miss Evans. And I thought it very nice of the gentleman to be so prompt, and he even gave me a little present for Twm there.'

'I wish he'd *told* me.'

My! She is in a state, he thought.

Twm looked out, their eyes met, and Cadi turned her head away, and he slammed down the window. 'We must go,' said Hughes.

'Of course, and thank you for everything, Mr Hughes. Sorry to have bothered you.'

It was with mixed feelings that she watched them reverse, and drive away, and followed them with her eye, all the way to the gate. And she was still angry. Why hadn't he told her about it? A sudden hole in the dyke of her independence. She walked very slowly up the hill, and saw the group coming down. She leaned against a tree, and waited for them.

'There you are, dear,' cried Lucy, 'wondered why on earth you ran off that time, we all did,' then, after a short pause, 'I thought it was very nice.'

'It was, and I was glad,' and in a moment she forgot all about a speedily settled account, and seeing her father's two old friends, her mood softened, and finally vanished. She hurried to them. How nicely they were dressed, how nice they'd been to her. 'Kind people, like the Edwardses.'

'We must be off now,' she said, gave then a smile to which they responded.

'Pity,' said Roberts, 'we'd hoped to have a little chat with you, Cadi.'

'I would have loved that, Mr Roberts, but my sister and her husband must really be on their way, a long way to go, and Lucy doesn't like the long drive in the dark.'

'Another time perhaps,' broke in Mr Phillips.

And Cadi wondered about that. She looked beyond the two men, and saw Stevens bent over a big tombstone, and Lucy standing behind him. She wished they'd hurry, she didn't want to keep her father's old friends waiting any longer.

She offered her hand to them both, and Mr Phillips took hers and held it tight for an instant.

'A sad occasion,' he said.

'And we'll be off, Cadi,' said Roberts.

'Goodbye now,' she said.

'Goodbye.'

'Bye bye,' cried Mr Phillips, and she watched them go, and waited for Lucy and her husband.

The two men waved to her from a distance, and she waved back.

'It was well worth it, and I never expected it.'

She made her way up the hill again. Stevens' voice hit the air, an excited voice, and as she drew near her impatiently waiting sister, heard him say, 'Do come and look, Lu, very interesting.'

'What is it, dear?'

'Come and *look*.'

'Lucy,' Cadi called.

'Just a sec, dear.'

'There,' cried Stevens. 'A Wellington man, Waterloo time, come and read it.'

Bent over the stone Lucy said, 'Yes, how interesting, dear. But we must get on now, mustn't we,' and pulled on her husband's arm, and louder, 'Here's Cadi, David; she's waiting.'

'Yes indeed, of course,' and they came hurrying to Cadi. 'Right,' he said. Stevens linked arms with them both, and they broke into a little run.

'Where's Mervyn?'

'He's in the car,' said Lucy.

'I'd give anything,' he said, 'for a nice cup of tea. Come along. Let's go.'

All three got into the car.

'Thank you again, Mervyn,' said Cadi, 'you were most helpful.'

'My husband thinks we ought to have a cup of tea somewhere on the way back.'

194

'Sorry,' said Mervyn, 'I must get back for the milking,' and it pleased Lucy.

'Of course you must, Mr Edwards,' and sharply to Stevens: 'And do let's move, dear, we're already delayed as it is.'

'It'd only be for about ten minutes,' Stevens announced, and to his disappointment there was no response.

'And you must allow for hold-ups,' warned Mervyn, already worrying about the time. It seemed to him that people like the Stevenses were rather casual, on all occasions.

'It's a long way,' were the last words that Mervyn spoke, and he settled himself comfortably into his seat.

The car moved off. Stevens kept a stubborn silence, and he was angry. A matter of ten minutes. What fuss, and he knew that what would have been even nicer was a pull up at the nearest pub. And how foolish of him to have left the flask behind, and he longed for it now. What a journey, what a strange funeral, and what a journey back. The wave of whispering in the back intrigued him. Mervyn quietly nodded off.

Cadi seemed interested in the man at the wheel; she studied his back, his head, he wasn't sat upright, but slumped back.

How disappointed he is, she thought. He'd have loved to stop for that cup of tea. 'What time is it?'

'Half past one.'

She turned to Lucy, lowered her voice. 'Glad it's over, dear?'

'We're all glad,' she replied. 'I didn't recognize Mr Phillips at all, but Mr Roberts, yes. What a good job you thought of them in the circumstances, dear.'

'Traffic beginning to thicken up again,' announced Stevens, but nobody appeared to be listening. What on earth are they whispering about back there. Odd the way Cadi left Lucy on her own like that, *very*, remembering, seeing her go, leave Lu entirely on her own. Why? Only complete strangers would do a thing like that, even that minister chap noticed it, saw him looking at both of them. I wonder if in some way they both felt a little guilty, perhaps so, and suddenly shy of each other. Could be.

Mervyn woke up, and Stevens looked at him, and was consoling. 'Long journey in a car, wish it was bigger, Mr Edwards, but we can't have everything, can we. I was worried starting off, my wife sometimes gets car sickness real bad. But something was merciful today.'

How they both fuss about one another, said Mervyn to himself.

'You've a pretty long drive ahead of you, Mr Stevens.'

'We have.'

Cadi heard, noted, and replied. 'Well at least we'll get back to a good tea, anyhow. It was good of Mari to do it, Mervyn.'

Mervyn laughed it off. 'Nothing at all,' he said.

'*What* an ancient looking vehicle that was,' Stevens said.

'Had it years and years,' replied Mervyn. 'I suppose it's the longest run Hughes has ever had. Take him a day or two to get over it.'

The women were silent, lost in their own thoughts, and Mervyn felt thankful that the driver had still forgotten the pipe in his pocket. From time to time he looked at the driver. There he was sitting there, and something against the grain on top of him. How grumpy he could be, and there was still a way to go. But then, cows were far more important at the

196

moment. Once or twice he even wished he could change places, let Mrs Stevens sit beside her husband, and Cadi and he at the back. After all they did have things to talk about.

'You were quite right, Mr Edwards,' Stevens said.

'Oh?'

'About the *snow*.'

And Mervyn stuttered it out, 'Oh yes, good job, too, and thank heavens for that.'

'What time is it now?' asked Lucy.

'Twenty to.'

'D'you think we'll make it, dear?'

'*Yes*.'

'Sorry we can't stop, Mr Stevens. Sure you understand, and I know you'd like a cup of tea.'

Stevens waved it away with, 'That's all right, Mr Edwards.'

'Mr Stevens?'

'*Yes?*'

'I feel your wife should be sitting here, not me.'

'Lucy?'

'What, dear?'

'Would you like to come and sit here, and let Mr Edwards go back there?'

'Stop the car,' Lucy said.

And he stopped the car.

'D'you mind, Mr Edwards?'

'Not at all,' and Mervyn was never more glad to get out, and unwind his six foot of man; he had been crouched there for hours.

'Everybody set?' asked Stevens, and turned to Lucy. 'Won't be long now, Lu.'

197

'I'm glad.'

Cadi was glad of the change, and Stevens noticed the renewal of a familiarity strangely absent during the journey. He supposed they had got things to discuss, and so indeed, had he.

'Lucy!'

'What, dear?'

'We can't leave before three,' he said, and then very close to her ear, 'wouldn't be right, Lu.'

'We've talked over that,' she replied.

'And I'm talking about it again, dear,' he said.

And a sudden whisper in his ear. 'Asked her again, and she won't.'

He turned to his wife. 'I cleared that up yesterday,' he said, 'and now, will you leave it *alone?*'

'Very well, David,' and then she looked round. 'You all right, dear?' Cadi said she was, but the uppermost thought in her mind was the curious exchange of whispers between Lucy and herself, a short conversation that had been most upsetting, after which they had remained silent. And, listening to it, she seemed barely conscious that the farmer was sat beside her.

'Cadi?'

'Yes, dear?'

'An awful thought just came into my head.'

'What awful thought?'

'Well, it's about Father, dear, and I suddenly asked myself a question, and I said to myself, "Have you once, in your whole life, ever asked Father how he was, if he was even *happy?*" And I couldn't remember.'

'How could you remember what you never thought of, dear,' said Cadi.

'It's still there, Cadi, and it's still awful.'

'There's worse things than that, dear.'

'Then don't tell me,' replied Lucy.

'The worst thing, Lucy, is when nothing, absolutely nothing happens to a person in a whole lifetime. Just think of that.'

But Lucy didn't, still puzzled as she was, still sad at the single thought that had shot up out of the blue. Now, she felt a little more comfortable, close to her husband. How concentrated he was, and how good a driver. It was a matter of pride with her that he had been so sensible about everything during that short but awkward stay. She lay back; she watched the telegraph poles fly by.

'We've certainly seen lots of Wales today, David.'

'We have indeed.'

'D'you think we can make Averton before midnight?'

'Before that, dear, I hope.'

'Yes.'

Talking for the sake of talking, thought Stevens, and he wished she wouldn't; he just wanted to be left alone, isolated at the wheel, lost in his own thought. Meanwhile the conversation in the rear was now incomprehensible to them both.

They're sat close enough together, thought Lucy.

When a suddenly accentuated word hit Stevens in the ear, he finally realized that he was listening to the language he had once heard back in The Gunner's Arms.

'Well, do think about it Cadi,' Mervyn said.

'Of course I will, but at the moment I can't seem to make up my mind about anything.'

'And you're determined to stay on there – alone?'

'Yes.'

'I see. But you must stay the night with us,' Mervyn continued. 'Mari asked me specially to bring you back this evening.'

Whatever would I do without these people, thought Cadi.

'Yes, all right then, Mervyn, I'll come back with you.'

'Good! Mari's leaving the bike at your place, and all I have to do is to nip home straight away...'

'You'll have a cup of tea, surely?'

Stevens listened to it all, and Lucy remained stonily silent.

'We must have a long talk about everything, Cadi. Tomorrow perhaps.'

'Yes.'

'I know where we are now,' exclaimed Mervyn, and called out to Stevens, 'we're almost there.'

Lucy sat straight in her seat, 'Thank God for that,' she said.

The nearer home they got, the more Cadi ruminated over the morning's surprise. Should she be glad about it, accept it, it *was* nice of Mr Stevens to do it, then again, it wasn't. Another little nip at what independence I've now got left to me. And what would Lucy think of that, her so generous David, all that money. Oh, I don't know, I don't, it just worries me. And what will Mr Hughes think about *that?*

'Another fifteen minutes,' said Mervyn, 'and I'll be out of this most uncomfortable little car.'

'But how handy it was,' said Cadi. 'And saved me having that one of Mr Hughes's.'

'True enough. But don't you feel cramped, Cadi; it's so tiny, isn't it?'

They both laughed, arousing the curiosity of Mr and Mrs Stevens.

Talking Welsh, Lucy thought, and then her eye gladdened to the first familiar landmark now come into view. Extraordinary. The last time I was in a car in these parts, was to meet David. It *does* seem such a time ago.

'There it is,' cried Mervyn, and Cadi gave out a little hurrah. Back. At last, the whole strange day now at an end, and her eye fixed on the chimney pot, and thankful to see the smoke rising lazily from it.

'Here we are,' said Stevens, loudly, and with a sort of magisterial tone of voice.

'I suppose we're all relieved,' said Lucy, and Stevens got up and rushed round to help her out, no mean feat in a confined space. Cadi herself was already through the gate, pushing in the door, seeing a well-laid table, a singing kettle, everything ready. She stood at the door, waited for them.

'All ready, come and sit down, oh, and take your things off.'

She ran upstairs. 'Shan't be long.'

'There's something under the door,' announced Lucy, and she picked up a note, well trodden on, that nobody had noticed. 'For you, Mr Edwards.'

'Thank you.'

'There's been trouble with the dog again, Mervyn,' he read, 'but don't worry. Tybaen and Arosfa are already out. And do have a cup of tea, dear, it's all ready.'

Cadi rushed down and served, and the Stevenses took their tea, and their eyes explored the table's contents.

'Good of your wife,' said Stevens, and picked up a freshly made scone. Mervyn smiled acknowledgement, but he did not sit down, spoke to Cadi.

'Must get back,' he said, and drank his tea standing up,

201

and refused the bread that was offered him. 'The bicycle's outside, Mervyn.'

'I saw it.'

The Stevenses rose, smiled at him, and each thanked him for the kindness received.

'Welcome,' said Mervyn, then turned to Cadi. 'Remember what I said, Cadi.'

'I will.'

'So long then,' and he departed with a chorus of so-longs behind him.

8

Stevens relished his tea, enjoyed the bread and butter. 'Lovely butter,' he said.

'Yes, and Cadi's giving me some to take home, David.'

'Good.'

The two sisters had been talking fast for the past ten minutes, but Stevens hadn't heard a word, but he had taken a last look at the kitchen, the narrow stairs, the tiny rooms, and what seemed to him so extraordinary was the absence of electric light. Would Pen y Parc ever achieve it? Another world, another life, and it wasn't for him.

'How old is this place, Cadi?'

'Three hundred years old, I'm told,' she replied. 'An odd name, isn't it. Pen y Parc.'

'You'd have to travel back three hundred years for the answer.'

'Cadi!'

Cadi leaned in, waited, wondered what might come.

'I wish in a way that we were able to stay the night, dear, but as you know David has his job to think about, and everything's a bit tricky these days.'

Cadi didn't know what 'tricky' covered, but she had the answer.

'I'll be staying the night with the Edwardses,' she said.

'Good,' said Stevens, and Lucy said how glad she was to hear that.

'Been thinking about it, dear, all the way back.'

'There's nothing to worry about,' said Cadi. 'More tea anyone?' Stevens waved it away but Lucy said yes, she'd like another cup. Stevens glanced at his watch, and Lucy went upstairs. They were alone. To his surprise Cadi reached across the table, and took his hand.

'*Thank you,*' she said.

'For what?'

'For what you did,' she said. 'Which reminds me, David, I've something for Lucy. I'll get it.'

From the big canister she took out a sealed letter.

'What is this?'

'Give it to her as soon as you get home. Not in the car, but when you get home.'

'What is it, Cadi?'

'An envelope, and what's inside it,' came her swift reply. Stevens took the envelope carrying the single name, '*Lucy*', and put it in his wallet.

'I'll remember,' he said.

'I'll slip up and help Lucy pack,' said Cadi, and left him seated at the table.

He lit his pipe, got up and collected his knapsack from the back. And he was ready the moment Lu said go.

He took another look round the kitchen, and ended up minutely examining the grandfather clock. I don't suppose she'd ever sell it. He reflected over the morning, the day before, the night of his arrival. How far away from everything these people seemed, how hard-working, an utter absorption, the sheer grind of it all. And the people he had met, he would remember the courtesy, and he didn't think it was something specially dressed for the occasion. He was glad he had come, seen, and even now was beginning to understand, which brought him back to Cadi. She had certainly worked, seemed never to have stopped. Had she ever seen the sea? Would she? And speculating. Might change her mind, come over, glad to have her. If anybody needed a change, she did. And Lu? How irritable they had been with each other, how distant, an awkwardness in the atmosphere, almost a coldness. If only something warmed it all up. He could feel the letter in his pocket, wondered what lay inside that note. He wished Mr Hughes had done the thing a little more diplomatically. Never mind. She had put out her hand, thanked him. He was pleased about that.

I'd never tell Lu, why on earth should I?

'I hope they won't be too long up there,' he said, and began to pace the kitchen. They'd hear him, know he was still around, and, like his wife, only waiting to go.

I'll write to Cadi when I get home. But I won't come back here, and Lu certainly won't.

He opened the knapsack, looked inside. Yes, the flask was there, and he put it in his hip pocket. And so was the bottle. What's keeping them up there, I wonder.

The two sisters were sat on the bed, and Lucy held Cadi's

hand. She wanted to *beg* Cadi to come over for a few days, but refrained. Hopeless. Three times asked, three times negative. What did that mean? Only one thing, a big no. A great pity. Wish she'd been more open, *really* talked to me, and how quickly she shut up about that missionary man she met. And it filled her with a curiosity that would never be satisfied.

'David's walking up and down, can you hear him, dear?' she asked.

'I can hear him. I don't want you to keep him waiting too long.'

'Listen.'

'I'm listening.'

Old ground again, thought Lucy, but I must, it'll be the last time. 'You know why I ran away and left him that time?'

'Of course I do, do we have to go over all that again?'

'No, dear. And I admire you for sticking it out, though I see no reason why you should have lost the boat. And there's still time, and I do hope something nice happens for you,' and she hugged her.

The stentorian call from below shook them both: 'Know the time?'

'Coming,' cried Lucy, 'shan't be long, dear,' and she got up, her hand still clasped to that of Cadi. 'And thank you for not reading that awful letter I sent him.'

Not again, thought Cadi, not *again*. 'Forget it,' she said, 'and your husband's waiting, dear.'

'Yes, I must.'

Cadi picked up her case, and preceded her out of the room. 'The butter,' she cried, and rushed downstairs and into the back.

'There you are, dear,' said Stevens. 'Must go now. Got everything?'

'Cadi's just putting in that butter. I'd have liked some cream, too, but I couldn't possibly ask for that as well.'

'No, you couldn't. Here she is.'

'Delighted to have it,' said Lucy, 'and now we *are* off. Ready, David?'

Cadi hesitated at the door. Should she go to the car, or stay there, and just wave as they set off. She changed her mind and followed them to the car.

'Goodbye,' she said, and shook Stevens' hand.

'Goodbye, Cadi,' he said, 'and it was nice to have met you.'

Lucy clung, saying, 'I'll write, dear.'

Cadi was silent, experienced a last embrace, and then her sister got into the car, not beside her husband, but having the back seat all to herself. She'd never forget that journey. And David simply must get another car.

Stevens dropped the window, put his head out, smiled, again offered a hand.

'Look after yourself.'

Lucy let down the window. 'And thank the Edwardses again for us.'

'Goodbye.'

'Bye.'

Cadi stood there as though dumb, heard the engine come to life, watched the car move off, a final wave when they waved, following them with her eye until the car disappeared out of the lane. She then returned to the house, and walked slowly up the path, pausing from time to time, for a wave of practical things had now obliterated all recollection of the departed visitors.

'Must tidy this up,' she told herself, and closed the door. She then did something she had never done before; she bolted it. She exploded into action, clearing the table, washing up everything, *opening* the little window over the sink, coming back again, *opening* the kitchen window, stopping to wind the clock, *noting* the time, half past three. She then went upstairs, and opened the windows in the two rooms. In the bigger one, she stripped down her father's bed, rolled everything into a bundle, and took it downstairs. Returning, she went straight to the chest of drawers, and *opening* the first drawer, she threw its contents to the floor, and so with the second drawer. At the bottom of the third drawer, she found an old newspaper, carefully wrapped, and inside it one hundred pound notes. She spoke aloud in the room. 'My wages,' she said, *and* evinced not the slightest surprise at her discovery, as though it had lain there, unseen, but nevertheless a right, and to be added to what lay in the big canister below. She sat down on the bared bed, stared round this room, and the eye missed nothing, object after object was noted, and finally her attention was suddenly attracted to the single book that lay on top of the chest of drawers. The permanent thing, it had always been there, and regularly she picked it up to dust beneath it, and put it back again. She took it to the bed, and sat down. Leisurely she ran its many pages to and fro, sometimes pausing to look at a heavily inked question mark in a margin, and occasionally to read an underlined paragraph. She knew it had always filled his room. The feel of it in her hand brought out the two words that she spoke aloud.

'Poor Father.'

And she remembered that the man who held it in his hand,

was a weak man who had his iron moments. She put it back on the chest of drawers.

Against the wall she saw the big black box, and bent down and opened it. It contained nothing but a big bundle of old newspapers, mostly the issues of a small Welsh weekly that arrived so promptly on every Saturday. She let the lid fall with a bang, then turned to what she had pulled from the drawers. Bending down, she examined everything, began bundling again, and eventually took everything downstairs. Something made her drop them, stand by the clock, listen.

Stevens liked this clock, and Lucy even suggested that I sell it. He was even interested in the vase, and going to the dresser, she picked it up. A huge vase. But is it Roman?

She looked at three shelves of plates on the dresser.

I used to put something in this vase every day of the week, yet it might never have been there at all, he didn't notice it, the colours in a kitchen.

It was nice of Tybaen and Treetops to send those wreaths. Reminds me I must walk the pig to Tybaen tomorrow, and she knew the boar would be waiting. And the cows can go out tomorrow. I must talk to Mervyn about the top field, too. She sat down in her father's chair, stared back at an empty one, thought of Stevens and Lucy. Calls her Lu. Nice old man. Glad I thanked him, and I still wish he hadn't, a lot of money. Will he eventually tell Lucy? Won't he? How sensitive she was this morning, not wanting to go through Penybont. Silly, after all that time, and why should anybody remember any of us. That line in Mr Roberts's letter really hit her, thinking of her father, reading the line again. 'We had almost forgotten him.'

Doubt if they'll reach Averton before dark. They *were* late departing. I told Lucy I'd stay on, and she didn't believe it, but I will. I'll alter things here, yes, I'll decorate the place, too. Her husband even had his eye on my dresser.

She collected two pails, and then went out for the milking, and it was like thinking of friends, and how glad she was that Miranda was now better. The weather was changing, she knew it would soon be spring. She thought of Mervyn calling for her at half past seven. A three mile walk in the darkness, and they would talk only of what mattered most, and at the end of which a long tedious journey in a car would seem only a memory.

She felt restless, uncertain, a wait of three hours. But he would come. She put on coat and scarf and suddenly left the house.

Seems ages since I walked to Paradise Corner, and yet it happened there only a few days ago. How odd, walking there now, and that's what I most want to do now. And I remember the very first time I ever went and sat in that spinney, a lovely summer morning it was, and I just slid away from the house, and saw Father making for the top field. I didn't know why, didn't want to, I just wanted to get away from the house.

The strong earth smells were in her nostrils, and she saw herself sat under the big sycamore, looking up at a blue sky, watching the endless passage of birds, drowsily, lazily under a tree.

And that's what I liked best, the solitude, and I was lost in everything about me. But it didn't last long. No.

Everything lost in a moment with the sound of heavy feet threshing through bracken, and before she realized it, a voice, and opening wide her eyes to the man that now stood staring down at her. The rude interruption, looking up, startled.

'Father!'

'Well?'

That awful shout. 'What?' I asked.

'*Work*.'

Half rising, coming out of a dream. 'Coming, Father.'

'Then *come*. And get that bloody scythe sharpened, too. *Yes?*' She remembered this, all the way to the spinney, where even the trees were lost in the darkness.

I wonder what made me come here, *now*, of all times?

And she stood there for a few minutes, listening, and there was no sound. Walking away, she knew that those quiet moments would never again be swallowed up by the loud voice of a man with the clock and the calendar in his head.

To no purpose.

She tightened the scarf about her head, clutched at the collar of the coat.

Why did he ever come to this place. And what made Lucy run from him?

Suddenly she was looking at her father, and he was stood alone in a near deserted railway station.

The things I said when I met him. 'What is the *matter*, Father?' And the things I didn't. I can see him now, so changed, not upright as I'd known him, but gone old, up-rooted.

From what had been anchored in him, his home, home that was *there*, seemed always so permanent, and purposive in her eyes.

Those letters.

She saw them burst into flame, so frightening her sister.

Perhaps there were more, perhaps there were reasons. Does it matter, now?

And *she* knew it didn't.

What I came to in this place brought me to ground. I bent to a new life, and seemed to sink further in and further down. We were both of us ignorant, knew nothing, but we learned in fifteen years. Yes. So I stayed, and gradually things I had been close to fell away, were no longer important. I gave up a school, and he gave up a home. And the order of those new days, in a strange place. When he said yes, I said yes, and when he said no, I said no. At first there was an anger inside me, but gradually it melted away. I quietened to, and accepted what was fixed. Knew he was wrong, knew I was (even cried in my mind) 'stupid', and in the end accepted it. I was sorry for him; I could never have said no.

She had reached the gate, and now leaned on it, staring up at the house.

What on earth am I standing here for?

And she hurried inside.

I was really sad when he stopped going to chapel, I almost froze when he told me, too surprised to answer. Sunday. A different day. I used to like Sundays, walking with him, going through the same door, sitting in the same seat, another world rising as we sat down, as we all sat, and listened as the words struck the air. How I remember that. She floated on words, and they carried her upstairs again.

I'll shift that bed now; I'll bring all my things here tomorrow.

She pulled, and she pulled again, at solid oak. Had it stuck to the wall, congealed? She knelt down, looked under the bed, and she knew it mustn't stay there; it must go to the other side of this room. 'It's the mattress,' she said, and bent to lift it, and then she was dragging it clear of the bed, and she thought of all the bed shaking and bed making of years, and the sweeping and dusting. And then it happened, for suddenly, soundlessly into her hand, like a leaf, there fell a small piece of cardboard.

What is it? and she let go the mattress.

A woman, and she knew the woman. It's her. And she took it to the window and looked at it again. Yes. Ty Coch days yielding up a secret. There she was, no change. Not his class, never could be. An elegant lady leading in her son's pony to be shod one morning.

And I saw her. And I saw her another time, both of them together, in the forge. I saw the solicitor's widow, and the lovely smile she wore, and Father staring, caught out. I ran away from it, couldn't believe it.

So she stood staring down at something she had long forgotten. Alive on a piece of cardboard. She flung it out of the window, and returned to the bed, took a firm hold, pulled on the mattress. The bed yielded; she pulled it clear, dragged it across the room, pulled away the big black box, steered the bed to the wall.

I'll change everything tomorrow, everything. I know I'm alone now, and I'm not afraid of it.

Standing at the top of the stairs, Cadi talking to Cadi again.

Was she the cause? Were they fleshed together on fugitive occasions, all that time back, when I was in Manchester, when Mother was still blind, was mouse, poor, simple, faithful Mother, Ty Coch's best servant, the one that was silent. Did she know all along, accept? Was *that* why he smashed up a home, after Mother died. Why he was *here?*

And down two stairs, and pausing again, being held in the scene.

Poor Mother. God! I wish I'd never gone to Manchester, *never.*

And the bottom stair, held, lost in this sudden upsurge of emotion.

And she knew it was too late to cry.

She cleaned out the fire, shovelled its contents into a bucket, took it outside and flung it into a ditch, after which she covered it with the damp soil. There was nothing more to do. And she wouldn't even bother to light the lamp. Instead she lit a candle, and stood it on the table beside her. The clock struck seven. He wouldn't be long now.

And she waited for Mervyn, and Mari sat and waited for them both.

Harry Hughes Williams (1892-1953) was born at Clai Mawr farm in Pentraeth, Anglesey. His family moved to Mynydd Mwyn, Llandrygarn in 1894. A childhood accident resulted in a disability which affected his mobility. He completed his secondary education at the Collegiate School in Liverpool and then the Liverpool City School of Art where he won the Prix de Rome, a European travelling scholarship he was unable to take up due to the outbreak of war. In 1914 he won a scholarship to the Royal College of Art in London, completing his education, then returned to Anglesey where he devoted himself to living and working as an artist. He exhibited at the Royal Cambrian Academy in Conwy and was elected joint member in 1921 and full member in 1938, when he also became art master at Llangefni Grammar School. He was lecturer to the forces during the second world war and exhibited throughout his life in galleries across Wales, London (including the Royal Academy) Liverpool, Paris, New York, Chicago and Boston.

N. H. Reeve is Professor of English at Swansea University. He has written widely on twentieth-century fiction and poetry, including critical studies of D. H. Lawrence, Elizabeth Taylor, and J. H. Prynne.

LIBRARY of WALES

The Library of Wales is a Welsh Government project designed to ensure that all of the rich and extensive literature of Wales which has been written in English will now be made available to readers in and beyond Wales. Sustaining this wider literary heritage is understood by the Welsh Government to be a key component in creating and disseminating an ongoing sense of modern Welsh culture and history for the future Wales which is now emerging from contemporary society. Through these texts, until now unavailable or out-of-print or merely forgotten, the Library of Wales will bring back into play the voices and actions of the human experience that has made us, in all our complexity, a Welsh people.

The Library of Wales will include prose as well as poetry, essays as well as fiction, anthologies as well as memoirs, drama as well as journalism. It will complement the names and texts that are already in the public domain and seek to include the best of Welsh writing in English, as well as to showcase what has been unjustly neglected. No boundaries will limit the ambition of the Library of Wales to open up the borders that have denied some of our best writers a presence in a future Wales. The Library of Wales has been created with that Wales in mind: a young country not afraid to remember what it might yet become.

Dai Smith

LIBRARY of WALES
FUNDED BY

Noddir gan
Lywodraeth Cymru
Sponsored by
Welsh Government

CYNGOR LLYFRAU CYMRU
WELSH BOOKS COUNCIL

SERIES EDITOR: DAI SMITH

WWW.THELIBRARYOFWALES.COM